THE MARVELOUS MS. MEDIUM

A LOST SOULS LANE MYSTERY

ERIN HUSS

Written by Erin Huss

Cover design by Sue Traynor

Author photo by Ashley Stock

This is a work of fiction. Names, characters, places, brands, media, and incidents are either the product of the author's imagination or are used fictitiously. The author acknowledges the trademarked status and trademark owners of various products referenced in this work of fiction, which have been used without permission. The publication/use of these trademarks is not authorized, associated with, or sponsored by the trademark owners...yada...yada...yada. Basically, don't sue me.

 Created with Vellum

PRAISE FOR ERIN HUSS

“Unpredictable and laugh-out-loud-funny!” **Readers’ Favorite** (*Making a Medium*)

“Erin has such a vivid imagination and is a great storyteller.” **Sheri, Amazon Reviewer** (*Making a Medium*)

“Hilarious and fun!” -**The Huffington Post** (*French Vanilla & Felonies*)

"Laugh-out-loud funny, and written in such a descriptive way that you could picture everything that was happening." **-Readers' Favorite** (*French Vanilla & Felonies*)

"This enchanting novel has hit a home run!" **Night Owl Suspense** (*Rocky Road & Revenge*)

“Simply hilarious!" -**Chick Lit Chickadees** (*For Rent*)

“Uproariously funny. Erin Huss is certainly one to watch!" - **InD'Tale Magazine** (*For Rent*)

“Five stars!”**- Cozy Mystery Book Reviews** (*Rocky Road & Revenge*)

"Fun! I highly recommend." **-KRL Reviews** (*Double Fudge & Danger*)

Silver Medal Winner in the International Readers' Favorite Awards. (*French Vanilla & Felonies*)

FREE BOOK

Sign up for Erin's newsletter to be the first to know about new releases, special bargains, and giveaways, and as a bonus receive a FREE ebook of the #1 Kindle bestseller, *Can't Pay My Rent*! erinhuss.com

ACKNOWLEDGMENTS

Thank you to my editor, Wendi Baker, you saved me; Sue Traynor for the cover; Paula Bothwell for being absolutely fantastic; Jed Huss for putting up with my grumpy moods when the characters in my head are not behaving as they should; Debby Holt, Ruth Bigler, and Jessica L. Randall for beta reading.

To my son, Fisher. You are funny, strong, fearless, and super hard to keep alive some days. I love you forever, and ever, and ever, and ever times infinity.

SERIES INFORMATION

If you've never read A Lost Souls Lane Mystery, you can start with MAKING A MEDIUM (only 99 cents), the first book in the series. If you prefer to start with THE MARVELOUS MS. MEDIUM (book #4), you won't be lost. Each book can be read as a stand-alone, but there will be a few spoilers should you read them out of order. I strongly recommend starting with book one.

You can get the first book at https://erinhuss.com Happy Reading!

CHAPTER ONE

Knock. Knock. Knock.

"Zoe?" Mike waves his hand in front of my face. "Are you going to answer the door?"

I feel a shiver of anxiety and shift to face him. We're sitting in my living room on the couch. My cat, Jabba, is curled up on Mike's lap, taking his midmorning snooze. "Yes. Just tell me *one* more time what will happen," I say.

Mike smiles, but I can see the muscles tense up a little in his jaw. Probably because this is the fourth time I've asked him to repeat himself.

"Brian is going to say he's happy that you're okay. Then you're going to say, 'Um ... um ... um ... um ...' Then he's going to say, 'Your job is waiting for you,' and you're going to say, 'Um ... um ... thanks ... um ...' Then he's going to say, 'I don't know about you, Zoe Lane.' Then you're going to do a nervous laugh, and he's going to kiss you."

My heart is galloping. Brian Windsor is the Editor-in-Chief of the *Fernn Valley Gazette* and my boss. He's also the most gorgeous man I've ever seen. "You're sure this is going to happen right now?"

Knock.

Knock.

Knock.

"Not unless you open the door."

I wring my hands. "What about Va-ness-a?" *Va-ness-a* is Brian's girlfriend. I'm unable to say her name without breaking it into syllables because I am jealous. Last I heard, she was moving back to Portland, but there was no word of an official breakup.

"Dunno about Vanessa," he says with a shrug. "Maybe Windsor is a player."

I seriously doubt Brian is the cheating type. "It's weird that I don't even ask him about Va-ness-a before we kiss."

"Dude, this is a *glimpse* of the future. It's not a full account. If you want to know what happens, just answer the freaking door."

Okay, Okay. "*Okay,*" I say, my butt still glued to the couch. "And after we kiss a spirit will appear?"

"Yes, like I've said, *several times*, a spirit will show up."

I shouldn't be surprised. Spirits appear all the time. I'm a medium. I can see and speak to the dead. Mike is also a medium. He has the ability to converse with dead animals, and he can catch *glimpses* of the future, which is how he knows Brian is waiting for me on the other side of the door.

Knock.

Knock.

Knock.

"Tell me more about the spirit."

Mike huffs a sigh. "Zoe, why aren't you answering the door?"

Because I'm twenty-three years old, and I've never had a real relationship, and the only person I've ever kissed is you, and I've envisioned being with Brian since I saw his editorial picture in the paper, and I'm worried he won't live up to the fantasy in my head, or even worse, that he will, but I'll lose him forever when he finds out that I talk to dead people ... is what I want to say.

"Because I want to be fully prepared," is what I actually say. Which is the truth. Typically, spirits appear and it's a scramble to figure who they are, why they're here, and how they died. It would be nice to have a heads-up. "You said we're going to help a mother who is looking for her daughter?"

"Dude, you are the worst procrastinator I've ever met. Answer the door already. I can't believe he hasn't left."

"I will, I will." I *will*. "But first, about this mother that we're going to help. Tell me more."

Mike first rolls his eyes then looks off into the distance. "The spirit is searching for her daughter who vanished twenty ... years ... ago ... I think."

"What do you mean *you think*?"

"The spirit appears, and you say she's been missing twenty years, and she thinks her daughter might still be alive ..." Mike squeezes his eyes shut and grunts. "I can't see the vision anymore. Why aren't my powers working?"

I put my frustration on hold and remind myself Mike is new to this. He'd known his whole life that he was different, but it wasn't until recently that he'd accepted the fact that he has paranormal gifts. I've been dealing with *my* gifts for about six months now, and I'm still learning how they all work. I shouldn't put so much pressure on him.

"Mike." I go to grab his hand, and Jabba hisses at me. *Guess I'll stay on this side of the couch.* "I don't think of our abilities as powers. What we have are gifts. And gifts don't always work as we want them to. They work as they're supposed to. Make sense?" I read that in *Hot Superheroes from Down Under*, and it resonated with me. Great book.

"It sort of makes sense." He opens his eyes. "I know there was a mother who was looking for her daughter, and I kept hearing you say twenty."

"And this mother shows up after I kiss Brian?" I know I sound like a broken record, but I want to be ready. If I'm prepared, then I shouldn't kill the moment by nervously rambling.

"Look, Zoe, I really like you. But if you ask me to repeat this one more time, I'm going to ..."

I wait for him to finish. But he doesn't. "You're going to what?"

"Probably nothing. Please answer the door."

Knock.

Knock.

Knock.

I start to stand then sit down.

Mike slaps his hands over his eyes. "If you don't answer the door, I will. But I'm not kissing Brian."

"No, don't do that. Just ..." I suck in a breath and blow it out slowly, regrouping. "Do we find the daughter?"

"I don't know."

My frustration returns. "What? How do you not know? What's the point of seeing the future if you can't calm my anxiety?"

"What happened to your whole 'it's not a power, it's a gift spiel? Give me a break. When I see the future, it's not like I'm watching a movie in HiDef complete with a full synopsis. The future comes in fragments, and it's like I'm looking through a foggy glass window. All I know is that we help a spirit whose daughter disappeared. Her name is ..." He brings his fingers to his temples. "Shoot. The vision is still gone. I'm pretty sure the name started with a J ... a Jo ... J-Jolene? Yeah. Jolene. Now, hurry up and answer the door."

"Okay, Okay." *Okay.*

Knock.

Knock.

Knock.

You can do this, Zoe. "I am standing up. I am walking to the door. I am not going to get weird. I am—"

"Taking forever," Mike cuts me off.

"Not helpful." I smooth down my hair, which is dark blonde and falls to my shoulders. I'm wearing sweatpants and a sweat-shirt, no makeup, and I'm pretty sure I'm rocking a haggard just-got-out-jail type of look. That's only because I did just get out of jail.

Falsely accused. Charges dropped. Long story.

"Dude, if you don't want to kiss Brian Windsor, I *fully* support that decision," Mike says. "I'd be more than happy to tell him you're not interested."

I gaze back at him. Mike Handhoff is a little older than me. Dark, coiffed mane, brown eyes. He wears his pants *really* tight, and he's a nice, funny, easy-going, and handsome guy.

"Are you okay with this?" I ask.

"With what?"

"*This.*" I gesture to the door. "You know, because of ..." I leave the sentence open, hoping he'll take over the conversation. We shared a passionate kiss not too long ago. My first kiss. Which is slightly pathetic given my age, but I'd been sheltered my entire life because my parents thought I was schizophrenic. I'm not. I just speak to dead people.

"Lane, listen to me. Open the door."

"Okay, Okay, Okay. Opening now," I say and grab hold of the handle. Deep breath in and, "*Gawk!*" I blurt out as I swing open the door. *You've got to be kidding me!* "Oh, look who it is, Mike!" I mutter through a clenched jaw. "It's *Mrs. Batch.*"

Mike scratches his head.

Here's what I know about Mrs. Batch: She looks like the See's Candies lady, is married to the mayor, and she plays Mrs. Claus in the Christmas parade. And she's one of the few people in town who believes that I am a medium and not a total nutjob. Which is why she asks me on the weekly to connect her with the deceased—most of which are cheating ex-boyfriends, evil dictators, or former presidents.

Also, she's *not* Brian Windsor.

"What can I do for you, Mrs. Batch?" I ask.

"Zoe, dear. I'm so glad you're home." She reaches into her purse. "I've added Mrs. Ishmael's cat to my list. Someone ran the poor thing over last year, and I want to know who it was."

"I can help with that!" Mike puts Jabba down and leaps over the back of the couch. "Speaking to dead animals is sort of my thing."

I cringe a little. Not because he can speak to animals. But because he's so open about his ability, and I am not. Even to people like Mrs. Batch who already know.

Mrs. Batch's mouth drops open. "Little Mike Handhoff can speak to the dead, too?"

"I sure can," he says with confidence, and I'm not sure why. He clearly hasn't perfected his gift, being as I'm standing here talking to Mrs. Batch instead of kissing Brian Windsor. I know these are gifts not powers, but talk about getting a girl's hopes up for nothing.

Mike escorts Mrs. Batch to the couch. "Can you also contact John Wilkes Booth?" Mrs. Batch asks. "I want to give him a piece of my mind."

I don't know how my parents—specifically my mother—would feel about us having a séance with presidential assassins in their living room. Not that it matters. Mike can only speak to dead animals, but still.

I go to close the door, when I see Brian walking up the driveway. *Oh my.* So it turns out Mike was a little off on the timing. No big deal.

Don't get weird, Zoe. Do not get weird.

Okay, I'm going to get weird. How can I not? I'm severely undersocialized, and ninety-nine percent of what I know about love comes from the hot romance novels stashed in my closet. I seriously doubt Brian will rip open his shirt, sling me over his shoulder, and take me to bed.

Right?

Crud. I haven't shaved my legs in a week. This isn't good.

"H-hi, Brian." I tug at the bottom of my sweatshirt. This outfit is quite possibly the most unflattering thing I own. Which is saying a lot, because I own a lot of unflattering clothes. "W-what brings you by?"

Brian pushes his glasses up the ridge of his nose—and what a gorgeous freckled nose it is. He has dark hair parted on the side with wisps around his forehead. Gray eyes with specs of brown in them. And he's at least a foot taller than I am. Also, he smells like fall leaves and orange zest.

"I came to see how you were doing," he says.

"I'm doing pretty good, considering." As in, considering I just got out of jail. But I don't want to bring that up right now. Incarceration is a total mood killer.

Brian shoves his hands into the front pockets of his jeans. "About Vanessa ..."

Aha. Va-ness-a. Here we go.

"We have officially broken up. She came this morning to get her stuff."

I remain stoic, but inside I'm doing a mental victory dance. "I thought she'd already moved back to Portland?"

"She had, but she came back last night and left this morning.

We're done." I catch a hint of remorse from Brian. Not unusual, I'm sure. Breakups are hard. Not that I'd know from personal experience, but there's at least one dramatic breakup scene in every romance novel I've read. They're quite emotional.

Anyway. Let's get to the kissing before this spirit shows up.

"It's been a crazy couple of months," Brian says.

"It sure has."

"Yeah."

"Yep."

He sighs.

I sigh. "Anything else you came to say?"

"Yes."

I run my finger around the collar of my sweatshirt, feeling hot in the cheeks. Probably because it's unusually stifling out today. I can already hear the ice cream truck melody down the street, and it's only eleven.

Brian takes a step closer, so close our toes are practically touching. My stomach is fluttering around like a swarm of drunken butterflies. Mike was right!

"I'm so happy that you're okay," he says.

This is it! Except, crud. What am I supposed to reply back with? Oh, that's right. "Um ...um ... um ... um ..."

"If you still want to work at *The Gazette*, your job is waiting for you." Not *exactly* what Mike said Brian would say, but close enough.

I want to say, "thank you!" But I mutter, "Um ... um ... thanks ... um ..." as to not stray too far from the script.

"I just don't know about you, Zoe Lane." Brian cups my cheek in his hand and stares into my eyes.

My mouth has lost the ability to form words, so I let out a nervous laugh instead and rise to my toes, closing the gap. Brian brings his lips to mine. They're warm and soft, and I can hardly believe that I am kissing Brian Windsor. Kissing!

I wrap my arms around his neck and tilt my head to deepen our connection, when there's a chill down my back and my fingertips go numb. *Gah!* Couldn't the spirit have waited two more minutes?

Brian pulls back. "Your face is so cold, Zoe." He uses the backside of his hand to check my temperature on my forehead. How this man hasn't figured out that there's something not quite *normal* about me by now is a wonder. He must be in denial.

I gaze over his shoulder, looking for the spirit Mike told me about. Typically, spirits who appear to me have just died moments before and are unsettled, trying to grasp the fact that they are now deceased. But I don't see a spirit anywhere. The neighbors across the street are watering their grass. The mailman walks by. A boy on his bike peddles down the street, and ... *ahhh*! I fall back, tripping on the porch step and land on my butt.

"What's wrong, Zoe?" Brian drops to one knee.

"I-I-I-I," cannot formulate a sentence. Mike was wrong. Mike was *so* wrong. Standing at the edge of the grass, spinning in slow circles, examining her hands is the spirit of *Va-ness-a*! As in, Brian's ex-girlfriend. She's dead, and she's here, and she's now staring at us.

"What are you doing here?" *Va-ness-a* runs to Brian's side. "Tell me what's happening. What is going on?"

Brian is still looking at me. "Zoe? Are you okay?"

"Look at me!" *Va-ness-a* demands. "Why aren't you ...?" She stumbles to the side and shakes her head. "Brian?" she tries again, her voice low.

Va-ness-a ... I should probably stop breaking her name up since she's dead and all. Vanessa is wearing a pair of light linen jogger pants that cuff at the ankles, a white shirt, and black heels. She's sporting the same choppy haircut as the last time I saw her, and she looks *even* prettier dead than she did alive.

"What the ...?" She examines her wrist. "Where is my tattoo? I have a small eternity symbol right there ..."

"Zoe, you're scaring me." Brian shakes me by the shoulders. "Are you okay?"

No! Your ex-girlfriend is standing here, dead.

I suck in a breath, attempting to regain my composure. "Brian, when Vanessa left your house this morning, did she say where she was going?"

Vanessa turns her head at the mention of her name and looks at me. "I've heard of you! You're the one everyone in town says is crazy. Can you see me?"

I nod my head slightly and realize Brian is talking to me. "What?" I ask.

"Why do you want to know about Vanessa?"

"Because I'm dead, Brian!" Vanessa claws at her neck and starts to pace. "I can't believe I died. I'm twenty-five years old. This is ridiculous. You know what? No. I am not dead. I refuse to be dead." She sits on the ground and crisscrosses her legs. "You are alive. You are alive," she chants, eyes closed. "You *will* live."

I don't think that's going to help.

"Zoe?" Brian takes my face in his hands. He's concerned that my short stint in jail has made me cuckoo. I know this because I can feel other people's feelings and I see their thoughts as they pertain to their current feelings. Brian is now wondering if everyone was right and I am the town crazy. Bless his heart, he's willing to stick around even if I am. I want to kiss him, but that would be awkward considering his ex-girlfriend is about five feet away, willing herself alive.

Gah! My life is weird. How the heck did Mike get this so backwards? Where is the mother looking for her daughter?

"Zoe," Brian says more firmly.

I peel my eyes away from Vanessa. "I-I'm fine. P-perfectly

well." I stand up. My legs feel wobbly. "When did Vanessa leave your house?" I whisper her name, not wanting to disturb her.

"It doesn't matter. We're over."

"Yes, I know. Was she upset when she left? Did she say she was going to meet someone?"

Poor Brian is so confused by my reaction. He's second-guessing whether he misread the situation and I don't have feelings for him at all. Which breaks my heart because I can't tell him otherwise. Not with Vanessa here. She just found out she's dead. I don't want to upset her more.

"Vanessa came to town last night to collect the last of her stuff, but nothing happened between us," Brian says. "We only talked, and then she left this morning to go back to Portland."

He's holding back important information. I can feel it. "*Nothing* else happened?"

"Nothing," he says. I don't believe him.

Something happened, but not necessarily last night. He feels guilty about an event involving money ... and a shore ... Vanessa and a shore ... *gah!* I can't get a clear picture, and it's freaking me out. What if he killed Vanessa?

"Did something happen between you and Vanessa regarding money?" I ask. "Something ... *criminal*?"

Brian's face goes gray. "Did you talk to her? Was she here?"

Was? *No.* Is? *Yes!*

"I haven't talked to her." Which is true. She and I have not had a conversation, yet. She's still willing herself alive. "Is there something you'd like to tell me regarding Vanessa and a shore?"

"No," he says, and he means it.

"What about the beach?"

Brian's face skews into a giant question mark.

Okay, so no money, no Vanessa, and no beach. Geez. Maybe both Mike and I need to work on our gifts.

"What was her state of mind when she left this morning?" I ask.

"She was *fine*. We parted on good terms. Why?"

Okay, phew. He's telling the truth. I can feel it. Plus, parting on good terms doesn't typically involve murder. "How about you call her," I say.

"Why would I call her?"

That's a good question. If I had been expecting my current love interest's ex-girlfriend instead of a grieving mother, then I might have had an answer prepared. As it stands—I got nada. Zero. Zilch. My mind is blank.

Pull it together, Zoe.

"Brian," I say, fidgeting with the bottom of my sweatshirt, not wanting to look him in the eyes. "I need you to check on Vanessa right now."

"Why would I do that?" He's so hurt and confused that I want to cry. I've been envisioning this moment for so long, and this is not how it was supposed to go.

"Please," I say.

"I don't understand, Zoe. Why are you so concerned about Vanessa?"

"I just want to be sure she's okay. *Please*."

There's a long pause, and I catch a hint of fear and guilt from Brian. There's an image of a body bag. *Ah!* Why is he thinking of a body bag? *Who* is in the body bag? *Dang it!* "She just left my house about forty minutes ago and was fine," he says.

Forty minutes is enough time to kill someone and stuff them in a body bag! Holy crap. I think I might faint. "Brian, I need you to leave." I manage to keep my voice steady and firm. I want him gone so I can talk to Vanessa and get to the bottom of this.

"If that's what you want." Brian shoves his hands into the

front pocket of his jeans. Jeans that hug his hips so deliciously I can't help but stare as he walks down the driveway.

I cannot believe I had to send Brian Windsor away.

He drives off, and my heart breaks into a million little pieces. No matter how awful I feel, Vanessa has to feel worse. I wipe at my eyes and take a seat on the grass, facing her. She's still chanting.

"Vanessa," I say. "Can you talk to me, please?"

"I will not be dead," she says, not opening her eyes.

"I'm very sorry, but you are dead," I say. "I'm here to help you transition peacefully."

Vanessa lifts her lids. "So that's what you do? You help ghosts like me who need to *transition*? What does that even mean?"

"When spirits appear to me, it's because they have business here on earth that needs to be tended to. I will help you tend to those things. Once you feel at peace, you can transition to the next life."

Vanessa is silent for a moment while she takes this in. "Why was Brian here?"

"Uh ... we work together."

"Why would he come on a Saturday?"

"Uh ... a story we're working on."

"Is this about the sheriff scandal?"

By "sheriff scandal" she means the last sheriff recently resigned because of a shady past that I uncovered. It's part of the reason I was in jail.

I don't want to lie to Vanessa, but I don't want to tell her the truth either. Not right now. Not when she's working hard to accept her death.

"He came to see how I was doing since I was recently released from jail after being falsely accused," I say. Which is absolutely the truth. Mostly. "Do you have any idea how you died?"

She shakes her head. "One minute I was in my car. Then suddenly I was here."

"Please concentrate. Do you think your death was an accident, or do you think you were killed?" I ask because I've learned that spirits might not remember the details of their death, but they'll have a gut feeling as to what happened. The first spirit to appear to me knew he'd been murdered, even if preliminary reports said he'd died of natural causes. The second spirit to appear to me knew she'd been hurt but wasn't dead, even if she didn't know who hurt her or where she was. The third spirit ... well, the third spirit was a mess. Anyway. I've learned to trust the spirit's natural instincts.

Vanessa stares off into the distance. "I know I was upset."

"Because you'd just ended things with Brian?" I ask, hopeful she'll say *yes* and not *no, I was upset because Brian was killing me!*

"No ... I mean, *yes*. But *no*. I was angry and anxious and scared. Emotions I don't typically allow myself to feel. Sure, I was upset about Brian. But there was something else. *Someone* else. I don't know who it was or what happened exactly, but someone else I interacted with caused my death."

Crap.

That sounds an awful lot like murder. Great. The last thing my little town of Fernn Valley needs is another killer. I'd already been involved in several murder cases over the last six months.

"Why can't I remember what happened?" she asks.

"Typically spirits don't remember their deaths. Especially if they were traumatic."

"Fan-freaking-tastic." Vanessa is up on her feet, biting her nails. "I left Brian's house around ten thirty. Put a bag of my stuff in the back of my car. I drove down the street. There was an ice cream truck on the corner and a group of kids lined up at the window."

Wow. I thought eleven was early for the ice cream truck to already be making the rounds. Ten thirty is still breakfast time. Also, it would be difficult for Brian to catch Vanessa, kill her, stuff her in a body bag, and drive to my house. Hallelujah!

Except—who was in the body bag?

Anyway. "The good news is that you couldn't have gone far," I say. The bad news is that Fernn Valley has a vast amount of wilderness. It would be very easy to stash a body deep in the forest.

"I cannot believe this happened," she says and starts pacing. "Do you know why I was in Fernn Valley in the first place?"

"To get your stuff from Brian's house?"

"No, not why I came here yesterday. Why I was here to begin with."

"I heard you came to win Brian back when your relationship was on the rocks." This was shortly after I started working at *The Gazette*. I'd seen her around the office a few times. This is the first time I've had an actual conversation with her.

"Vanessa Tobin doesn't uproot her life to *win* a man back," she says.

So I guess her last name is Tobin. Good to know.

"I came for a story." Vanessa stops pacing and lets out a loud gasp. "Do you know what this could mean?" She looks at me expectantly, and I shrug. "It could mean I was close. Too close. Dammit. I must have been close."

I don't follow. So I say, "I'm not following."

"I work for *The Portland Times*, and I've been investigating the disappearance of a twenty-year-old college student from Portland."

I had no idea Vanessa was a journalist. But most importantly, "Did you just say *twenty*? As in she's been missing *twenty* years?"

"No, Lux Piefer was twenty *years old*, and she disappeared *six* months ago. The last place she was known to be alive is here in Fernn Valley. I've been digging around over the last two months. Do you think I struck a nerve, and someone killed me before I could uncover the truth?"

Not sure. I'm still stuck on the *twenty*. What are the odds that Vanessa was working a missing person case for a *twenty*-year-old? Sure, there's a big difference between missing twenty years and being twenty years, but still. The coincidence is too much of a coincidence to be a coincidence, coincidently.

"Zoe?" Vanessa snaps her fingers in front of my face, except they don't make the snapping noise. "You there?"

I blink a few times, trying to refocus on Vanessa. "Do you *feel* like the reason that you're dead is because you were close to uncovering the truth about what happened to Lux?"

"I'm not sure." Vanessa clenches her jaw and stares up at the sky for a while. Then, with slow determination, she nods her head. "Yes. I *feel* like the last person I talked to is the person responsible for the disappearance of Lux Piefer. I *feel* like I had uncovered who it was, and that is why I'm dead. I'm sure of it. Dammit!" She goes back to pacing. "How the hell did I figure it out so fast? I talked to Lux's mother last night, and we were going over leads, but there wasn't anything solid. I remember leaving Brian's house, but I don't remember knowing what happened to Lux."

"Maybe you didn't figure it out until the person was killing you?" I offered.

"Aha! That could be it. Or it came to me while I was driving. I'm pretty brilliant when it comes to this stuff."

And humble. "Vanessa, you said you spoke to Lux's mother last night. So she's alive, right?" I ask.

"Yes, she lives in Portland."

"Are you sure she's alive?"

"Very sure. She's going to be devastated when she finds out that I died. Crap. I can't believe this has happened!"

"What is Lux's mother's name?"

Vanessa stops pacing. "Jolene Piefer ... Are you okay? You look pale."

"Only that ... um ... excuse me, I need to have a conversation with someone. Right away."

CHAPTER TWO

I run inside.

Mrs. Batch is on the couch dabbing her eyes with a handkerchief. "You have a gift, Mike." She pinches his cheek.

Not wanting to totally ruin the moment, I clear my throat until I grab Mike's attention. When his eyes meet mine, I jerk my head, motioning for him to come.

"We were having a moment," he says, following me down the hallway. "You're not going to believe what I was able to do. Dude, I legit talked to a cat, and you're not going to believe who ran him over."

"It was Mr. Sanders."

Mike frowns. "How'd you know?"

"I saw his thoughts once. He feels terrible, but it was an accident." I pull him into the bathroom. "We have a huge problem right now."

"Windsor is a bad kisser, right? I knew it. Don't be disappointed, Lane. Not everyone can live up to me—"

I shush him. "Vanessa showed up."

"Was there a fight?" He sounds way too excited about this. "Who won?"

"No, Vanessa's *spirit* showed up."

Mike scratches his head. "Wait, she's dead?"

"Very."

"And she's here?"

"Yes."

"She's the spirit who arrives when you're kissing Brian?"

"Yes."

"Dang, Lane. That's harsh. She dies, and then she has to watch her ex making out with her medium."

"She didn't see us kissing. I don't think." Surely she would have mentioned it.

"Did you tell her that you have the hots for Brian?"

"No, and I'm not going to."

"Yeah, that's not going to backfire."

"Is that a vision or a personal opinion?"

"It's a personal opinion."

"Then keep it to yourself." I feel a bit restless and moody. Could be because I just sent Brian Windsor away so I can help his ex-girlfriend catch her killer, or catch Lux's killer, or ... *Ugh*. There are too many dead, or missing, or whatever people. "I thought a mother was supposed to show up. What happened?"

Mike stares off into the distance, and I wait anxiously. "I don't know," he finally says.

"That is *really* unhelpful."

"I'm sorry. When I had the vision, I saw Brian and you kissing, and then a spirit showed up. I couldn't see the spirit, but I knew the spirit was there based on what you said. The spirit's name was Jolene, and her daughter was last seen alive in Fernn Valley, and you said '*twenty years*.'"

"Is it possible that the spirit in your vision *was* Vanessa, and she and I were talking about Lux Piefer who is *twenty years* old?"

"It was a mother. I'm positive. I couldn't see the spirit, but I could sense the spirit. She was older, and it wasn't Vanessa. When she showed up, you told Brian you weren't feeling good and asked if you could call him later."

That is certainly not what happened. Not at all. "Turns out that Vanessa is a reporter, and she's been investigating the disappearance of *twenty*-year-old Lux Piefer. She was last seen alive here in Fernn Valley *six* months ago. Her mother's name is *Jolene*. That can't be a coincidence."

"Dude, you're saying that Jolene knew Vanessa?"

"Yes. Somehow Vanessa appeared instead of Jolene. According to Vanessa, Jolene is very much alive."

"Dude. How'd that happen?"

My honest opinion is that Mike saw the future wrong. He did second-guess himself on the *twenty* before I'd even opened the door. It's completely maddening, but not totally his fault. He's still honing in on his abilities. I know firsthand how hard it is to figure out how these gifts work, and I don't want to discourage him.

"It doesn't matter how it happened," I say. "It matters that it did. Now we have Vanessa here with us. She thinks the last person that she talked to is the person who is responsible for Lux's disappearance."

"What do we do now?"

"We need to ditch Mrs. Batch and find out what happened to Vanessa," I say.

"Cool. Let's go."

I swing open the door and stumble back into Mike, who falls into the bathtub, taking the curtain with him.

Vanessa is standing in the doorway, balancing on one leg with her hands clapped together and eyes closed.

"Is she here?" Mike whispers, still lying in the tub.

"Yes," I whisper back and help him up.

"What is she doing?"

"She's standing in the doorway."

"Why?"

"I don't know."

Vanessa lifts her arms over her head and rises to her toes, stretching her long body. "Accept what you cannot change. Change what you cannot accept," she says.

"What's happening?" Mike asks.

"Not sure."

Vanessa lowers her leg, and she crosses her hands over her heart. "I have chosen to accept my death." She opens her eyes. They're a beautiful sea blue color with specs of green. "I *cannot* accept that I died without closing the Lux case. That's not how Vanessa Tobin is going out. Vanessa Tobin is going out an award-winning journalist."

"Wow. You've won awards for your articles?" I ask.

"No! That's the point. I *do* work for *The Portland Times*. I'm not necessarily a journalist *at The Portland Times*. I'm an office assistant. Paying my dues, so one day I can be an award-winning journalist who travels the globe, uncovering the injustices of the world, and empowering women. This Lux story was my shot! It's part of an exposé I was writing. Even though Jolene filed a police report, Lux's case went seemingly untouched by the police. This happens *way* too much. Do you know how many mothers are out there looking for their missing adult children with no help from the authorities?"

I shake my head.

"Thousands! Chances are Lux is dead. I was going to find out what happened to her, submit it to my editor, and it was going to be my big break. I knew it. Now what? I just die an office assistant whose greatest accomplishment was making coffee *for* the award-winning journalists? You said that I have to finish my earthly business before I can transition. *Lux* is my earthly business. We find out what happened to her, we finish the article, we turn it in to my editor, and I will be remembered as the talented journalist who died while doing something important. Then I'll transition to wherever you want me to go."

Geez. This was a tall order. Sure, I've helped spirits find out how *they* died, but I've never helped a spirit find a missing person and write an award-winning article about it. Yikes. "Don't you want to find what happened to *you*?" I ask.

"If we find out what happened to Lux, chances are we'll find out what happened to me. Are you in, or are you out?"

It's not like I can say no.

"Of course I'll help," I say. "Come in." She steps into the bathroom, and I close the door behind her. "This is Mike, and he's a medium as well. Part of his gift is the ability to see glimpses of the future."

"That's fantastic," Vanessa says. "Except we need to know what happens in the *past*. Can you see the past?"

"Wait a second." Mike lifts his chin and tilts his head. "I can *almost* hear her words."

Oh good. I dreaded having to repeat *everything* Vanessa says. "Focus." I grab his face, forcing him to look at me. "If you can communicate with animals, I'm certain you can communicate with human spirits."

"Yeah. You're right." Mike bounces around on the balls of his feet, cracks his knuckles, then gets into an odd stance, like he's about to enter a limbo competition.

Uhhh. "What are you doing?"

"Getting ready to listen. Go ahead. Tell her to say something."

Vanessa shrugs a *this guy is odd but what do I have to lose* sort of shrug and puts her mouth up to Mike's ear. "The rain in Spain!"

"Yes!" Mike does a fist pump. "It's raining in Spain? I got it! "

Vanessa and I share a look then shrug a *close enough* type of shrug.

"You'll get the hang of it," I say.

"Dude, I can communicate with humans *and* animals. I'm totally crushing this medium thing."

"I'll give him this—he's confident." Vanessa leans against the counter and crosses her arms. "Now, back to my earthly business. Let's start the basics of the case."

"Slow your roll," I say. "There are a few things we need to go over. First, we need to talk about Brian. When he was here earlier, I felt his feelings and saw his thoughts."

Vanessa's eyes widen. "You can read minds?"

"No, I can feel other people's feelings and see their thoughts as they pertain to their current feelings."

"Have you ever read *My House, My Hexagon*?" Vanessa asks.

"Zoe only reads books with naked guys on the cover," Mike pipes in. Guess he's getting the hang of hearing Vanessa.

"That is not true." I do have a few covers with half-naked men who are holding puppies, because variety is good. "Anyway. I haven't read the house ... whatever. Is it a children's book?"

Vanessa laughs as if I just told a joke. "It's by Dr. Luisa Fandan. She's a life coach. You should read the book because it will blow your mind." She mimics a head explosion. "There's a chapter all about thoughts and feelings. She says that what you think is how you feel. If you're thinking about sad things, then you're feeling sad. If you're thinking about happy things, you're feeling happy. If you're thinking about an upcoming dental appointment, you're feeling anxious, or scared, or happy if nitrous oxide is your thing. My point is that thoughts and feelings are directly connected. So it's not that you can see people's thoughts as they pertain to their feelings. It's that you can see people's thoughts, period. Because thoughts cause feelings."

Dang. She's right. My mind is blown. I should go the library and check out the hexagon book instead of the Cocky Bahamas Guys series.

Or, I could get both.

Probably both.

"Now, back to Brian," says Vanessa.

"Right. He was feeling guilty, and he was thinking about a shore. When I asked if he'd ever done anything criminal, he didn't answer. Then he thought about a body bag." I gasp. "What if the person in the body bag is Lux?"

"Dude, Windsor wouldn't kill anyone," Mike says. "There's no way he'd get his hands dirty. And I mean that figuratively and literally. Have you ever seen that guy's office and car? He's a neat freak."

Yes, Brian's office always smells of Lysol, and his car is immaculate. At least it was, until I totaled it that one time I was being chased. Long story ... Anyway, he has a new one now, and I'm sure it's equally clean.

"Mike is right," Vanessa says. "I don't think Brian killed Lux. I didn't think he'd dump me either. Maybe you're on to something."

I really hope I'm not, but I can't ignore what I felt from him.

"He was never supportive of my investigation," she says. "Said there was not enough information and no one in Fernn Valley had anything to do with her disappearance. He refused to help, which wasn't like Brian. He loves a good missing-person case."

This is true. Brian does love a good mystery. Dang it. I really don't want Brian to be a suspect.

"Dude, Windsor is *not* a killer," Mike repeats.

"Well, he saw a body bag," I say. "So somebody died."

"What exactly happened to this Lux chick?" Mike asks.

"Not a chick. She's a woman. And I'm glad you asked." Vanessa points to the ground.

I grab Mike by the hand and pull him down to the floor beside me.

"What did you do that for?" he asks.

"Vanessa said to sit. So we sit."

"I need my laptop," Vanessa grunts. "I have a Lux file with everything on it, but it's in my car. We need to get that, asap. My article is on there, too. Anyway. Here's the short of it. Lux Piefer is our victim. She was twenty years old, and she attended Oregon State as a photography major. She had taken the semester off to travel. She had been home for the weekend and told her mother that she was driving down to San Francisco to stay with friends. She stopped here in Fernn Valley to stretch her legs, fell in love with the charming community, and decided to stay the night and explore the town more the next day, take pictures, and check out the local hiking trails. Are you still hearing me, Mike?"

Mike nods.

"Good. Lux last spoke to Jolene around five o'clock that day. She told her mother about her plan to stay the night and explore the town the following morning before driving down to San Francisco. Jolene called Lux later that night, and she didn't answer. She called the next morning, and still no answer. Her texts were going unread, which was not like Lux. She and her mother were very close and talked often. Lux wasn't terribly active on social media, but her last post was of a book festival here in town."

I raise my hand.

"Yes, Zoe?"

"I was at that book festival."

Vanessa just stares at me. "*And*?"

I slowly lower my hand. "And ... that's it. I didn't see anything or ... anyway. Continue." *Geez.*

For the record, it was a lovely event. Local authors had set up booths with their latest books. Butter Bakery sold delicious treats, and there were balloons and banners and pendants and cotton candy and ice cream. It was a scene fit for any Hallmark movie. Knowing Lux was there and disappeared shortly after sort of puts a damper on the memory.

"Jolene filed a missing person report, but nothing ever happened," Vanessa continues. "The police's position was that Lux was an adult who was traveling. They promised to look into it, but they haven't done anything. Jolene knew something was wrong, and they completely dismissed her. She came here to Fernn Valley to look for Lux, but she wasn't able to find anything. It's like Lux vanished into thin air."

Mike raises his hand.

"Yes, Mike?" Vanessa says.

"Is it possible that she did take off?"

"No. She would have contacted her mother by now. The two share a cell plan, and Lux has not used her phone once since the day she disappeared. She hasn't withdrawn any money from her bank account either."

I raise my hand.

"Yes, Zoe?" Vanessa says.

"Did Jolene use the Find My Phone feature to see where Lux was?"

"Excellent question. The last place Jolene was able to trace the phone was here in Fernn Valley, around Earl Park where the book festival was being held. She checked with the Fernn Valley lost and found, and she looked all over that park. The phone wasn't anywhere."

Mike's hand goes up.

"This isn't kindergarten. You can speak without permission," says Vanessa.

"Got it." Mike lowers his hand. "Did you ever involve Sheriff Vance?"

Ugh. Sheriff Vance. Just his name makes me instantly nauseated.

Here's what I know about Sheriff Vance: He was the sheriff of Fernn Valley for pretty much ever until recently. He resigned because I uncovered a decade-old secret that ruined his career and life.

"Yes," Vanessa says. "Jolene filed the missing person report with the Portland PD, and she spoke to Sheriff Vance. The sheriff wasn't all the interested in solving the crime. We now know it's because he was too busy dealing with his own problems."

I start to raise my hand then remember we're not doing that anymore. "You said you were close to solving the crime. What do you think happened?"

"Another excellent question. I think Lux attended the festival, and I think she asked around to see where she could stay. There is only the one hotel, and it was booked. Jolene and I logged into Lux's Airbnb account, and we found that she had last searched for a place to stay here in Fernn Valley, but there wasn't one. Under normal circumstances, I'd say she gave up and left town. But her phone was last here in Fernn Valley. I think she might have slept in her car, and someone found her, and they killed her. The thing is, Lux could have been dumped in the forest. But the killer would have had to get rid of the car. The tow company is run by some shady men. They could have easily had something to do with this."

My eyes slide to Mike. Based on his expression, he's thinking the same thing I'm thinking.

"My dad owns the tow company," he says. His voice full of regret.

"Your last name is Handhoff?" Vanessa practically spits the words out.

Mike's eyes are swiveling as if looking for the nearest exit.

"He's nothing like his father," I say, breaking the awkward silence. "Nothing at all. Mike is a wonderful guy."

Vanessa studies Mike under intense scrutiny, trying to decide if she can trust him.

Here's what I know about Mike Handhoff's father: His name is Stephen, and he's currently in jail for a number of crimes—dealing drugs and burning down the Self-Storage Place, being a few of them. He also owns the tow company and impound lot.

"You said that you felt like you were talking to the person responsible for Lux's disappearance when you died. Stephen Handhoff is in jail right now. He couldn't have been involved," I say.

"Sure, but who is to say there wasn't more than one person involved? I've been coming to Fernn Valley for almost two months. I tried getting information from him before he went to prison, and he refused to help with my story. Now his brothers run the business, and they're equally unhelpful. Sounds to me like they have something to hide."

"I could talk to my dad," Mike adds as if an afterthought.

I can tell he'd rather not face his father.

"No, I'll do it," I say. "I can *read* his mind."

"No, Zoe. You don't need to do that," Mike says.

Vanessa shushes him. "Stop trying to be heroic. Zoe is a strong woman. She can do this. Plus she has better powers."

"I don't know about *better*," I say. "Being able to see the future is pretty cool." Even if he can't see it quite right yet.

"What we need to do is find *my* car," Vanessa says, ignoring me. "I want my phone and computer. All my information from the Lux case is on there. That should be priority one."

"I think there's a good chance you were involved in a car accident since the last thing you remember is being in a car thirty minutes before you showed up dead," I say.

"If you were in an accident, your car would have been towed and kept at the tow yard," says Mike. "We can go check if it's there and talk to my uncles. Kill two birds with one stone."

Vanessa gives Mike a look. Not that he knows this, because he can't see her. "Poor choice of words given there are likely two dead women in this case," she says.

"Sorry." Mike starts to shrink then bolts upright. "If Lux is dead, Zoe can contact her!"

"Yes!" Vanessa snaps and points at Mike. "Excellent idea. You're forgiven for your idiotic idiom," she says then looks at me. "Well?"

"O-o-okay." I wet my lips, my stomach a bundle of nerves. The thing is, Vanessa is a wee bit intimidating. I *really* don't want to let her down. "I'm not *that* great at connecting to spirits. They mostly just appear to me."

"Listen to me, Zoe," Vanessa says, her voice firm. "Saying you can't do something is a cop-out. You need to believe it and do it. Mind over matter. Don't make excuses."

Actually, I didn't say I *couldn't* do it. I said I wasn't great at it. Like Mike, I'm still perfecting my gifts. But whatever.

I hug my knees to my chest, close my eyes, and envision a door. The door is surrounded by light, and I call for Lux and wait. When a spirit has transitioned to the afterlife, I can't see them. I can only feel their spirit and see their words. Even if Lux hasn't transitioned yet, I should still be able to reach her.

Come to me, Lux. Come to me, Lux. Come to me, Lux.

I see the outline of a woman walking through the door. She's waving her arms around as if to say *no!* She doesn't want to talk to me.

Please come to me, Lux. Please come to me, Lux. Please come to me, Lux, I mentally say instead, hoping if I'm more polite she'll come.

No such luck. The outline disappears, and the light around the door fades.

Wow. I've never had that happened before.

I gaze up at Vanessa, who is staring at me anxiously.

"She's dead," I say. "I saw the outline of her spirit, but she doesn't want to talk to me."

"Why the hell not?" Vanessa asks. "Doesn't she want us to find out what happened to her?"

There's a knock on the door, and we all freeze.

Oh gosh, I completely forgot about Mrs. Batch. Heaven knows what she thinks Mike and I have been doing in the bathroom together for this long. In hindsight, my bedroom would have been a less awkward place to congregate.

"Why is she here?" Vanessa asks.

To connect with a pet, Mike mouths the words.

There's another knock on the door. "Are you two okay in there?" Mrs. Batch asks.

"We'll be right out," I say sweetly then look at Mike. "Finish with her so we can go."

"Dude, this is super heavy stuff. I can't connect with anyone right now."

"Put that crap in an emotional receptacle and face the forward without un-conviction," Vanessa says.

Mike and I say, "Huh?" in unison.

"Haven't you read *The Lubox Theory*?" she asks.

We shake our heads.

"It's an excellent book. I don't have time to explain. Just stuff the receptacle and go."

"Uh ... sure." Mike gives me a *what does that mean?* look and opens the door. I stand beside him, and Mrs. Batch's eyes bounce between the two of us.

"You do make a handsome couple," she says. "I wonder what powers your children will have?"

Oh, geez.

Mike ushers her to the living room. "Let's resume our session on a different day. Shall we?"

I can hear Mike still talking to Mrs. Batch when I turn to Vanessa. "I can't ignore what I felt from Brian." No matter how much I want to.

Vanessa's brow is wrinkled. "I have no idea what you're talking about. The most unpredictable thing that man has ever done is dump me."

"How long were you two together?"

"Since freshman year of college."

Oh, gosh. I had no idea they'd been together so long.

The awful truth is, I don't know Brian well at all. We've worked together but not closely. I know that he's attractive, and he smells heavenly, and that he likes carrot cake with cream cheese frosting. I know his uncle died earlier this year. I know he had a girlfriend. That's it. I don't even know where his house is. I suspect it's not too far considering this is Fernn Valley. "Brian moved here to run the paper and be close to his uncle," I say, thinking out loud. "And you decided to stay in Portland. So you had a long-distance relationship for ... what? A couple of years?"

"A year and a half." Vanessa sounds a bit annoyed. I can see her thoughts. She wants me to concentrate on Lux, not on her relationship with Brian.

"Why didn't you move here to Fernn Valley when Brian did?" I ask.

"Because there was nothing for me here. Brian and I had

planned to stay in Portland, but then right before graduation, he announced that he was going to Fernn Valley to take over the—no offense—most boring paper on the planet and to be near an uncle that he didn't even know that well. It was very un-Brian like to make such a drastic decision."

Interesting.

A month ago, I wouldn't have even entertained the thought of Brian as a suspect. But both spirits and people who I knew a lot better than I know Brian have burned me. It's hard to know whom to trust. All I know for sure is that Brian is hiding something. Something regarding a shore and a body bag, and he *feels* guilty. What if Brian killed Lux, stuffed her in a body bag, and dumped her in the ocean?

Also, he was the last known person to see Vanessa alive.

I hate that I'm even having these thoughts.

Vanessa is quietly tracing an infinity symbol on the inside of her wrist, the spot where she mentioned her tattoo was. All this talk about Brian is resurfacing feelings Vanessa would rather not think about. She's mentally chanting *emotional receptacle* to stop herself from dwelling on their breakup. She loved him. She trusted him. She's hurting, and I feel like crap.

I feel like crap because while she was dealing with the loss of her life, I was kissing the man who broke her heart.

"Why an infinity symbol?" I point to her wrist.

"I lost my grandmother about two months before my college graduation. She was shot during a home burglary. Infinity symbols were our thing. My mom had a lot of emotional issues, and she left when I was a kid. My grandmother—*her* mother—was the closest thing I had to a mom. I used to worry that she'd leave me too. But she'd tell me how she wasn't going anywhere and that she loved me to infinity." She continues to trace a figure eight on her wrist. "I got the tattoo a few weeks ago."

My heart aches for her. "I'm sorry. I don't know why the

tattoo would disappear. At least you can see your grandma soon."

"Yeah, well. We'll see." She's back to mentally chanting *emotional receptacle.*

Mike returns. "Mrs. Batch is gone, and I had a thought. Vanessa, did anyone ever talk to Mr. or Mrs. Ishmael?"

Vanessa shoves thoughts of her grandmother and Brian and tattoos into her receptacle. "The people who own the dry cleaner?"

"Dude, they also do boarding at their house. I was just talking to Mrs. Ishmael about it this morning because I'm homeless."

Mike had been living with Sheriff Vance. Being as Mike and I had uncovered the sheriff's lies, it would be a little awkward for him to still be living there. Speaking of which ...

"What about Sheriff Vance?" I ask Vanessa. "Do you think he had something to do with Lux's death?" I've read the sheriff's thoughts many times, and I've never seen a twenty-year-old girl. However, that only means he wasn't thinking about her. "Do we know where Sheriff Vance is?" I ask.

"He left town a few days ago," Mike says.

Oh. "Doesn't mean he wasn't involved, though. Like Vanessa said, it could have been a two-man job. Do we know where he went?"

"I heard he's hiding out in Nevada until the gossip dies down."

"He's still a suspect on account of he's a highly suspicious person," I say. "Mike, text around and see if you can get more of a definitive answer on his location."

"Aye, aye."

"Can we *please* stay on one topic at a time?" Vanessa asks. "I had no idea Mr. and Mrs. Ishmael offered boarding. Where do they live?"

"They live really close to the dry cleaners and Earl Park," he says.

"Fantastic. How long have they been doing this boarding thing?" she asks.

Mike shrugs. "I'm not sure."

"Okay." Vanessa holds up her pointer finger. "Step one is we go to the tow yard to see if my car is there. Being as I'm invisible to everyone but Zoe, I can easily look around to see if Lux's car happens to be there as well. Then Mike can ask to speak to his uncles, and Zoe can read their thoughts to see if they had anything to do with Lux. She had an old, gold Honda Civic hatchback. It's an ugly and hard to forget car. Look for that in their thoughts. Step two depends on if my car is there or not. If it's not, step two will be finding my car. We need my laptop and my phone. Step three is talk to the Ishmaels. Jolene never mentioned them. I think it's safe to say she didn't know about the possibility that Lux could have stayed there. Step four ... Are you seriously texting someone while I'm talking?"

I look up from my phone. "No. No. *No.* I'm writing down the steps."

"Why?"

"In case we forget?"

"Vanessa Tobin *never* forgets."

Good to know.

"Step four and five will depend on what we find. Step six is solve murder. Step seven is publish my article. Step eight is win awards. Step nine is transition. Got it?"

"Dude, I'm new to this whole solving crimes thing. But doesn't it take more than nine steps?"

"Pfft." Vanessa waves her hand as if there were a fly buzzing around her head. "I believe I already figured out what happened to Lux once today. I'm sure I can do it again. Let's get going.

Where is your car, Zoe?" Vanessa walks through the wall then pokes her head back in. "Found it. Come on."

Mike runs a hand through his hair. "This is ... is ..."

"Stressful?"

"No."

"Ulcer-inducing?"

"Nah."

"What were you going to say then?"

He smiles. "Exhilarating. Dude, we could solve a crime, Zoe."

Oh, poor naive Mike. He has no idea what he's in store for.

"Can I drive?" he asks.

"Nope."

"Worth a shot."

CHAPTER THREE

"Keep your eye out for my car," Vanessa says from the front seat. She made Mike sit in the back because she gets carsick. He didn't want to point out that spirits don't get sick and humored her.

To everyone else, it looks like I'm chauffeuring Mike around. A bummer for him, being as the back seat of my car is tiny, not constructed for anyone over five feet.

"I would have had to drive down the frontage road," Vanessa says, looking out the window. "Check for disturbed bushes or tire marks."

"We could go to Brian's house after the tow yard and retrace your last steps," I say.

Mike grunts, and I check the rearview mirror. His knees are near his ears. "You doing okay?" I ask.

"Just peachy," he mutters under this breath. "Can you turn off the heater, though? I'm dying."

"Oops. Sorry." Even though Fernn Valley is currently experiencing record high temperatures, I'm freezing. This is what happens when I'm around a spirit.

"How do you have such a nice car?" Vanessa asks. "This

thing had to cost close to a hundred grand. *The Gazette* doesn't pay that well."

No, it doesn't. The BMW i8 was a present from the first spirit I helped. It has butterfly doors, runs on both electric and gas, and its masculine body turns heads. Especially since there are key marks on the driver's side door and *bith* is scratched into the passenger side door—a not-so-nice parting gift from a criminal who couldn't spell. When you get yourself involved in murder cases, you put the people and things you love in jeopardy.

Which gets me thinking.

"You don't think Brian is in danger, do you?" I ask.

Vanessa throws up her arms. "Why in the world would he be in danger? Honestly, do you have ADD? Last we talked, Brian was a *suspect*."

"Yes, I *know*. But if he wasn't involved in Lux's death, do you think whoever did kill Lux would come after Brian thinking he might know something?"

"Good news for him is he wanted nothing to do with the Lux case, and he wanted to cut all ties with me and go our separate ways so he could date other people," says Vanessa. "The killer would have no reason to go after him."

Mike's earlier comment about my relationship with Brian backfiring comes to my mind. Probably because he's in the back seat quietly chanting, "Backfire, backfire, backfire."

I shoot him a look then concentrate on the road. We don't have time to deal with whatever is happening between Brian and me. And, truthfully, I'm nervous about going to the tow yard. The last time I crossed one of Mike's relatives, he tried to light me on fire.

I grip the steering wheel and drum my thumbs along the stitching, trying to calm my nerves, when my phone rings and a number flashes on the dashboard screen.

Oh, no.

"That's Brian's number." I can feel Vanessa staring at me. "Are you going to answer?"

"Uh ... sure." I accept the call. "Hello, Brian."

"Zoe, can we talk about this morning?"

"No. I don't want to talk about this morning. Not now."

Vanessa eyes me suspiciously.

"I'm sorry if I offended you," he says.

"I'm not offended. Perfectly ... um ... un-offended." Is that even a word?

"About Vanessa ..."

"Oh, we don't need to get into that."

"Yes, we do," snaps Vanessa. "Ask him about the body bag. Why are you being so goofy?"

"I'm not goofy," I whisper.

"Dude," Mike interrupts, thank goodness, because this is not going well. He leans forward, between the two front seats and talks to my dashboard. "Why didn't you want Vanessa investigating this Lux girl's disappearance?"

Oh, geez. I cannot believe he just came out and asked him.

"Is that Mike?" Brian asks.

"Yes," I say, understanding how this might sound to Brian. I give him the brush-off so I can hang out with Mike. "We're working."

"On the Lux Piefer story? Why?"

"Tell him that you know me and you want to help," Vanessa says. "Then tell me what he's thinking."

"I can't see thoughts over the phone," I mutter under my breath.

"Don't say *can't*." Vanessa pounds her fist into her palm. "Say *can*. Put all doubt into the receptacle."

"Okay, but I *cannn ... ttttt* see thoughts unless I'm next to the person." Also, I'm super confused as to how this receptacle thing works.

"What was that?" Brian asks.

Oh, geez. There are too many conversations happening right now.

"Brian," I say. "Let me call you back later." I end the call. Wow, that was stressful. Luckily he didn't say anything about our kiss this morning.

"Why didn't you tell Brian that you know Vanessa is dead?" Mike asks.

Vanessa rolls her eyes, as if she is offended by Mike's stupidity. "My death is of none of his concern. I'm not his girlfriend anymore. He made that perfectly clear last night. We got in a huge fight."

This is new. "What did you fight about?" I ask. It's hard to imagine Brian ever losing his temper. He's so even-keeled.

"He accused me of being brash and pushy. Two things I am absolutely *not*. I am bold and assertive. There's a difference."

Is there?

"I called him an unimaginative Mr. Rogers," she adds.

"Hey, what's wrong with Mr. Rogers?" I ask.

“Nothing ... I was mad." She shifts her focus to the window. "If I'd known that I was about to die, then I would have been nicer."

"There are far worse things to be called than Mr. Rogers. He was wonderful, happy, and a kind man," I say, trying to comfort her, but she's back to reciting *emotional receptacle* and doesn't hear me.

We take the rest of the drive in silence. Me concentrating on the road. Vanessa concentrating out the window. Mike concentrating on making himself as compact as possible.

The tow yard is located on the outskirts of town, next to the remains of the Self-Storage Place. A chain link fence wraps around a lot full of cars that have seen better days. I park at the curb. Mike climbs out of the back seat and stretches his arms, touches his toes, and twists his back.

There is a sun-worn trailer with a walk-up service window near the entrance to the yard, and we wait behind Tanner Ishmael, who is arguing with a woman who has a beehive of red hair and pink lipstick.

"You can't force me to pay for my car," he says. "That's against the law."

"It's not against the law, honey. And you know it." The woman has a cigarette between her two fingers and takes a drag. "You parked in a handicap spot." She blows out a circle of smoke.

Here's what I know about Tanner Ishmael: He's Mr. and Mrs. Ishmael's son, and he's in his late twenties with a shaved head and brown eyes. He's a jack-of-all-trades. I've seen him around town working at his parents' dry cleaners, making donuts at Butter Bakery, driving the snowplow in the winter, cleaning the gazebo at the park, and he dresses like the Easter Bunny during the spring festival. Not sure if he's married or if he has kids, but he does only wear shirts with sayings on them. Today it says *Duct Tape Can't Fix Stupid, But it Can Muffle the Sound.*

Also, he parks in the handicap spot.

"There weren't any other parking spaces, and I do have a busted leg." Tanner points down to the bandage wrapped around his calf.

The redheaded woman in the window is not impressed. "Honey, the car was towed, and now it's here. You can have it so long as you pay. That'll be one hundred and twenty-five dollars."

"What! That's ridiculous. Did you detail it while it was here? Dip it in gold? Install rims made of diamonds? One hundred and twenty-five dollars!"

Mike decides to intervene. "Dude, she adds an additional five dollars every time you yell at her. I'd suggest paying now."

"Well, well, well, well," says the woman. "Look what the cat dragged in. It's little Mikey Handhoff."

He waves. "Hi, Aunt Berthy."

"You look good, kid."

"Thanks."

Tanner moves his hands around helplessly. "Sorry to interrupt this little family reunion, but I need my car. I have to get to the dry cleaners."

"That'll be one hundred and thirty dollars then."

Tanner looks like he's about to implode. Then he shoves his hand into his pocket and pulls out his wallet. "You take cards, right?"

Aunt Berthy points to the sign in the window. *Cash Only*.

"What!" Tanner kicks at the ground, making a dirt cloud.

Mike puts a hand on Tanner's back. "I've got you, bud." He pulls out his wallet and takes out several twenties. "Pay me back at practice Monday."

Tanner hesitates, staring down at the money. I catch a feeling of skepticism from Tanner. He and Mike are on the Fernn Valley Softball team. They've always been friendly, but Tanner isn't so sure about Mike anymore. His dad did burn down the Self-Storage Place, which ticked off a lot of residents who had items stored there. And his aunt is holding his car hostage.

Ultimately, he decides to take Mike up on his offer since he doesn't have any other choice. "Thanks, man." He grabs the cash. "I'll pay you first thing Monday."

That's a lie.

Tanner doesn't get paid for another two weeks.

Gah! I really miss the time when the only feelings and thoughts I had were my own.

"I know you will, dude," Mike says. "While you're here, let me ask you about your parents. Your mom says they do boarding at their home. How long have they been doing that?"

"Why? You going to stay with us?"

"Ask if Lux stayed there!" Vanessa yells so loudly that I almost fall over. She'd been so quiet, for a moment I forgot she was here.

Tanner runs his eyes over me, thinking about what a shame it is that someone so fine is so crazy. Wow. "You good? Or is it time for your medication?" He laughs.

I do not.

Neither does Mike. "Not cool, dude. Not cool at all."

"Sorry, man." Tanner holds up his palms. "Didn't mean to offend. It's just ... what are you doing hanging out with the town nutjob?"

"This coming from a man who can't even match his socks," Vanessa says, and I look down. He's wearing an off-white, mid-calf sock on his right foot and a white anklet sock on his left.

Mike cracks his knuckles. "As a matter of fact, she's not crazy. Not even a little. But if I ever hear you call her crazy again—"

"Okay, that's enough." I step in. "There's really no need to talk about crazy this or crazy that. It's not a competition. We're all a little off our rockers. Do your parents keep a record of who has stayed at their house?"

Tanner blinks. "Are you for real?"

"Yes, I am for *real*. Answer the question."

Tanner stiffens. I don't have a good feeling about him. His spirit isn't dark, but it's not light either. There's something not quite right there. He's thinking about how he doesn't want to talk to me because he thinks I'm crazy.

Mike opens his mouth, and I place my hand on his chest.

"Hold on." I turn to Tanner. "Put your hands behind your back and hold up as many fingers as you want."

"What?"

"Just do it," Mike says. "Or I take back the money."

"Fine," Tanner grunts and puts his hands behind his back.

"You're holding up two fingers. Now three, four, ten," I say. "Now you're flipping me off. Seven, two, eight."

Tanner checks over his shoulder to make sure there's no mirror behind him. He doesn't see Vanessa, who is telling me exactly how many fingers Tanner is holding up.

"Also, I know that you're behind on your rent and you have no plans whatsoever to pay back Mike." I step forward and rise to my toes so we're almost eye level. "I know you hurt your calf this morning when you accidentally sliced your skin with scissors, trying to get the gum you got stuck in your leg hair. I know you snatched the gum from your mom's purse last night when you took twenty dollars from her wallet. It's a blue wallet. She's had it since you were a kid. I know you're feeling a little freaked out because you heard I was a medium and psychic, but you assumed I was crazy, but you're beginning to think that I'm not so crazy after all. And you'd be right. I am not crazy. I can feel your feelings and read your thoughts, and if you call me crazy again, I'll blurt all your secrets to the entire town, and you, Tanner Ishmael, have a lot of embarrassing secrets. Got it?"

"Bravo." Vanessa is clapping her hands in slow, rhythmic, soundless motions. "Bravo!"

Tanner is completely dumbstruck, and I feel a stab of guilt. I would never blurt out his secrets to anyone. "Do your parents keep records of everyone who has stayed at their home?" I ask.

"Yy-es," he stutters.

"We're looking for information on a twenty-year-old woman named Lux Piefer," I say. "She was here during the book festival, looking for a place to stay. The hotel was booked. Do you know if she stayed at your parents' house?"

Tanner gulps, and his mind goes a bit spastic. There are glimpses of balloons, and candy, and the ice cream truck, and the gazebo. I think it's the book festival from his perspective. I see familiar faces, and a cotton candy machine, and me sitting on the curb reading a book then a girl with dark skin wearing a red baseball cap with a ponytail of black hair cascading out the back. She's taking pictures of the gazebo with a large camera. She's slender, and young, and beautiful, and Tanner had never seen her before. He talks to her. It's obvious she's not interested in him, but she does ask if there are any other places to crash around there besides the hotel. Tanner tells her that his parents offer boarding and they live close.

"What happened to her?" I ask.

Tanner takes a step back. "I don't know what you're talking about."

"Yes, you do. I saw your thoughts." I turn to Vanessa. "Was Lux African-American?"

"Yes, she was," Vanessa says. "She was tall and had long, beautiful hair."

Aha! The girl in Tanner's thoughts *is* Lux.

"W-who are you talking to? Dude, stay out of my head." Tanner tosses the money at Mike. "I'm good, man. I'll get my own car out ... uh ... later."

"Dude, just tell us what you know," says Mike.

Tanner backs up towards the street. "I don't know anything."

It's hard for me to tell if Tanner is freaked out because he knows what happened to Lux or because I'm reading his thoughts. Either way, he's already running down the street. Guess his leg feels better.

"Should I go after him?" Mike asks.

"No," says Vanessa. "We need to stick with step one."

"But he met Lux," I say. "He told her that his parents offer boarding."

Vanessa blinks. "Then why the hell are we just standing around? Go get the man!"

The three of us take off running. Tanner has already disappeared. He either went left into the forest or right, going towards town.

Time to split up. Mike goes left. Vanessa and I go right. I'm running along the side of the road as fast as my legs will take me.

"Do you see him?" I ask Vanessa.

"No. Not anywhere. What a little twerp."

"At ... least ... we ... know ..." *Gah!* Never mind. I can't run and talk at the same time. What I'm thinking is that we know Lux likely stayed at the Ishmaels' home, or at least she tried to.

Ouch! I'm paralyzed by a side cramp and fall to my hands and knees. *Sweet mother ...gah!*

"What are you doing?" Vanessa stomps her foot "We're going to lose him!"

"Sorry. I ... I can't ... move."

Vanessa grunts and throws her hands up in the air. "Stop saying *can't*. You *can* move."

Her whole *rah-rah you can do this* attitude was a lot more charming when I didn't feel like my intestines were on fire. *Gah*! This hurts.

"You need to breathe more when you run," Vanessa says.

"I'll ... keep ... that ... in mind." I try to move, and my body says *nope*.

"Dr. Ludwisk says it's vital to encapsulate your pain and work around it."

I stare up at Vanessa who is standing over me, giving me the most pitiful look, and say, "Huh?"

"It's from the book *Winning Your Sensations*. You're

supposed to identify the cause of your pain, put it in a capsule, and work around it."

So pain goes in a capsule and emotions go in a receptacle? I'm not entirely sure how this is supposed to work. All I know is there isn't a capsule or a trash can big enough to hold what I'm currently feeling.

"Zoe, are you encapsulating your pain?"

"Sure." My phone rings from the front pocket of my sweatpants, and I check to see who is calling. "Oh, good. It's Mike. Maybe he found Tanner." I slap the phone to my ear. "Hello?"

"What's wrong? Are you hurt?"

"No. I'm putting my pain in a capsule. Did you find Tanner?'

"No, I didn't. But I had another vision, and it's not good."

Oh, no. "Mike saw the future again," I tell Vanessa and put the phone on speaker. "Go ahead, Mike. Vanessa can hear you now."

"We're in a forest," Mike starts.

Vanessa crouches down. "Stop breathing so heavy," she tells me. "I can't hear him."

I close my mouth and breathe through my nose.

"We're all there," Mike says. "It's dark, and there are loud explosions and gunfire. A man with mud on his hands has a gun pointed at Zoe. The vision is too foggy, I can't see the man's face. But he fires a shot. A woman wearing jeans and a blue shirt jumps in front of Zoe, takes the bullet for her, and dies. That's all I see."

"Fantastic," Vanessa says in a way that implies it's everything *but* fantastic. "Who is the woman?"

"I don't recognize her," he says. "I think this happens tonight."

"Tonight," I choke out. "How do you know?"

"Because you're wearing the same outfit, and I just ... *know*."

"Hold on." I manage to sit upright. "What do you mean *bombs* and *gunfire*? Did a war break out?"

"I have no idea. All I know is that we're in Fernn Valley."

Holy hell! I think I may pass out.

"There's more," he says, and I put my head between my knees. "This morning, it was supposed to be Jolene instead of Vanessa. I'm sure of it. Sure, I may have been wrong about the twenty years old versus the twenty years missing. But that's only because in my vision you said *missing twenty years*."

He's right. Well, I mean, I didn't meet Jolene. I did, however, say *missing twenty years* out loud when I was talking to Vanessa. Shoot.

"What if the future is ever changing?" says Mike. "What if Jolene was supposed to die this morning, but something happened and Vanessa died instead?"

Mike's realization makes the hairs on my arms stand up.

"I'm lost," Vanessa says. "How was Jolene supposed to die this morning?"

I tell her about Mike's initial vision—minus the whole Brian and me kissing part.

"Jolene is in Portland, and I was in Fernn Valley," she says. "How could I have died instead of her? Does the person responsible for Lux's death have the ability to teleport? And that's a totally serious question, by the way. I mean, you can speak to the dead. Mike can see the future. I'm sure there are people out there who can do even cooler things."

Teleporting would be a fun gift.

"If what Mike is saying about the future is true, then something we do causes explosions and gunfire and a woman to take a bullet for me." Who would do that? The only person I can think of is my mom. But she doesn't wear jeans, and Mike knows what she looks like. It couldn't be Jolene. I don't know her, and she's in Portland. Even if she left now, she wouldn't make it here in time to become a human shield. Not if this happens today!

"Uh, Zoe?" Mike says. "What kind of car does Vanessa drive?"

"Tell him I drive a Toyota Corolla, four door with Oregon State license plates," says Vanessa.

I relay this information to Mike.

"You're going to want to get over here quick. I found her car. It's smashed into a tree. I'm along the highway, going north towards Trucker County."

The highway? That's like a two-mile run. Dang. Mike is obviously in better shape than me. Pretty sure we've covered about a quarter of a mile. If that.

"Yes! We can get my laptop and phone." Vanessa takes off running back towards the tow yard.

I scramble to my feet and race after her, trying to put the pain radiating through my body in a capsule.

CHAPTER FOUR

We decide to drive the rest of the way and not run. Thank goodness, because I haven't mastered the receptacle/capsule/hexagon/whatever method. Fifteen minutes later, we're nearing the county borderline. There are a few emergency vehicles along the side of the road, but we don't see Vanessa's car.

"Wow. You took out the town sign." I point to the *Welcome to Fernn Valley* billboard that is now lying flat on the ground.

"Pull over. Pull over. Pull over. Pull over," Vanessa chants. "Over. Over. Over. Over."

"Okay. Okay. Okay." I park behind a fire truck getting ready to leave, and Vanessa disappears.

I scramble to get out of my car and struggle to my feet. The i8 is fun to drive, but it's hard to get in and out of. Gracefully that is.

Mike is waiting for me behind a different fire truck. "We have a problem," he says as soon as I approach.

Great. "What happened?"

"I just remembered the new sheriff is Mr. Executer."

I couldn't possibly have heard him right. "Executer?"

"Yes, Executer. He was my high school drivers ed teacher. He took over as sheriff until a special election can be held."

"Okay, what's his deal? Is he a psychopath like the last sheriff?"

"No, but he didn't like me."

"Why?"

"Because I crashed his car a few times during driver's training."

"A few?" I squeak. "And you wanted to drive *my* car?"

"I was sixteen. How about you take the lead on this?"

Will do.

As we approach the scene, the fire trucks drive off and a Handhoff Towing truck pulls up with the lights flashing. A man with a slicked ponytail of black hair and sunken cheekbones jumps out of the driver's side and slips on a pair of gloves.

"Is that your uncle?" I ask Mike.

"Yep. I have two uncles. Frank and Gary. Frank is a pretty reasonable guy. He's married to Berthy. Gary likes to play with guns."

"Is that Frank or Gary?"

"Gary."

Great.

"I'd rather not confront him right now with questions regarding Lux," Mike says. "He's not happy with me. It'll be better to do it at the tow yard with Frank around."

"Why is he mad at you?"

"He thinks I'm responsible for my dad's arrest."

"Your dad burned down the building. How was that your fault?"

"My family is weird."

Weird is one word for it. "How'd you turn out so normal?"

"You think I'm normal? I just had a twenty-minute conversation with a dead cat this morning."

Sounds normal to me. "If we want to get Vanessa's stuff from the car, we shouldn't let anyone see us anyway."

"Good call."

We step aside and take cover behind a different bush. It's there that I spot Vanessa's car, which is smashed into a tree like an accordion. Vanessa is already at the scene, fluttering around the vehicle.

Mike and I walk down the embankment and through the brush, careful not to slip. With each step, the presence of a dark spirit grows stronger. "Do you feel that?" I whisper to Mike.

"What am I supposed to be feeling?" he whispers back.

"A dark spirit."

He pauses mid step. "No. What does it mean when you feel a dark spirit?"

"It means there's a bad guy here." I check to see if Tanner is around, and my eyes land on Gary. He's inspecting the *Welcome to Fernn Valley* sign now lying on its side, kicking at the broken post with his toes. A grin spreads across his face. The grin doesn't conjure up happiness; it's sinister and senseless and *dark*. I'll need to get closer to him to see his thoughts.

But first, we have to get Vanessa's laptop and phone. She's frantically searching through the vehicle, pulling at her hair, and muttering to herself.

"She's by the car," I tell Mike. "Now she's waving for us to come down."

We check to make sure no one is looking. Coast is clear. We take off and hide behind the tree Vanessa's car smashed into, which is a massive oak tree that towers at least fifty feet. "Does this forest look familiar?" I ask.

"No. The one in my vision is full of pine trees."

I make a mental note to stay away from pine.

Vanessa appears in front of us. "My purse, phone, and laptop are all gone."

"Is your body there?" I ask.

"No. They already removed me."

Dang it. "They could have grabbed your personal effects and kept them with your body," I say.

"There's also a fudge pop wrapper and stick on the passenger seat that was not there before."

"You said you saw an ice cream truck this morning," I say, suddenly remembering. "Did you stop to get a fudge pop?"

"I'm lactose intolerant, and it was too early in the morning for dessert."

"Do you think someone else was in your car, eating a fudge pop?" Mike asks.

"Honestly?" Vanessa cocks her thumb. "Where did you find this guy? *Yes*, Mike, that's exactly what I was saying."

"Be nice," I warn. "And you're sure the wrapper wasn't there before?"

"Positive."

Vanessa did feel like the last person she talked to was the person responsible for Lux's disappearance. If that person was in the car eating ice cream, wouldn't they have died in the crash, too? But if Vanessa doesn't do dairy, then where could the wrapper have come from? At least we have one potential clue. Sadly, neither Mike nor I have the ability to identify DNA—that would be a cool gift, though. Because I'm sure there are fingerprints or saliva on that wrapper that could lead us to the person responsible for all this. Even if the police were to take the wrapper into evidence, they'd have to send it off to be tested. That could take weeks. We don't have weeks.

We have hours.

"What are you two doing here?" intones a male voice. Mike and I spin around. It's Elvin Peterson.

Here's what I know about Elvin: He wears bowties and fedoras and squints when he talks. I've had very few interactions with him, but I know he lives in Fernn Valley and works in Trucker at the paper there.

"We're here to ... um ..." I look to Mike for help.

"Write an article," he says.

Oh, that's good. "What are you doing here?" I ask Elvin.

"Same." He holds up a small digital camera. "Darn shame. Fatal car crashes don't happen too often around here. When they do, they usually involve a deer, a tree, or a phone. This gal was messing with her phone while driving. I hate when young people die."

Me, too.

I turn to Mike. His mother was killed in a car crash when he was young. Elvin's words and the sight of the car smashed into a tree bring on a wave of grief, and I can feel Mike fight hard to keep these emotions at bay. I slip my hand into his to let him know he's not alone with his feelings, that I'm here, and even though she wasn't my mother, I feel his grief, too.

Honestly, it's a beautiful moment we're sharing.

Until Vanessa starts cursing.

"I don't touch my phone while I drive," she howls. "Ask him how he knows this!"

"How do you know the victim was on her phone?" I ask.

"I was told that she was swerving on the road while messing with her phone."

"Who told you?"

"He cannot publish that in the paper!" Vanessa shouts in my ear, and I jump. "That will ruin my credibility. I want people to know that I died while uncovering the truth! I was not some distracted driver!"

"Uh ... uh ... listen, Elvin." I let out a little *hey we're all friends here* type of laugh. "Vanessa was also a reporter, and I think ... um ... out of respect for both her and her family, it would be best if we don't mention how the accident happened."

"Yeah, that's not happening." Elvin sounds as if there's a wad of mucus stuck in this throat. "The first thing people will ask when they read about a fatal car crash is *How did this happen?* It's a good reminder to stay off your phone."

"Dude, what will it take for you not to publish this?" Mike asks. "Like, come on, it's not cool to call out the dead like that."

"*Dude,*" Elvin says, mocking Mike in his phlegmy voice, "I'm just doing my job. Isn't that what you're doing? Don't you owe it to the public to give them the truth?"

Vanessa goes back to cursing.

She does this for a while, fluttering around the trees. "We need my phone to see who I last contacted. I must have been talking to the person who killed Lux! That's why I was distracted. That's why I was swerving!"

Then who was eating ice cream?'

"Do you know if her personal belongings were taken with her to the coroner's office?" Mike asks Elvin.

Elvin snaps a few pictures. "What do you want with her stuff?"

"She's a friend," I say. "That's all."

"Not sure. I just got here too. You can ask the sheriff. He's coming this way."

I can hear the leaves crunching and feel the presence of the sheriff approaching. I'm beyond relieved when the spirit is light and friendly and overpowers the darkness surrounding this crash. Sheriff Executer—despite his unfortunate last name—is nothing like his predecessor.

Phew.

"Michael Handhoff," comes Sheriff Executer's soft voice. "What are you doing out here?"

Mike and I turn around. "We're friends of the victim," he says.

Sheriff Executer is younger than I anticipated. Early fifties, with a full head of blond hair and eyes so light blue they're almost see-through. His skin has the look of someone who burns at the sight of the sun, and I can tell by the way his uniform hugs his arms that he works out.

"I'm sorry for your loss," he says with a sigh. "Unfortunate accident. I hate to see young people leave this earth too soon."

"I like him much better than the old sheriff," Vanessa says. "Ask him how he found my car."

"How did you find the vehicle?" I ask.

"We received a call. Said she veered off the side of the road and plowed through the welcome sign. We rushed to the scene, but she was already gone."

"How do you know she was on her phone?"

The sheriff knits his brows. "Where did you hear that?"

I point to Elvin, who is behind the car taking pictures.

Sheriff looks heavenward and wipes the sweat from his brow. "He shouldn't be sharing details. Not until we've spoken to the family. But, yes, off the record, the nine-one-one caller was driving behind her and said she was swerving and on the phone. Coincidently, her cell was still in her hand when we found her."

"Don't you think she would have dropped her phone when she drove down the embankment?" Mike says. "Wouldn't she have gripped the steering wheel and pumped the brakes?"

"You would know how one handles an accident," he says to Mike. "Worse student I ever had. But you turned out okay, kid." He gives Mike a friendly smile. "Glad to see you out of jail."

"Me, too."

Me, three.

But there's no time for small talk. "Who was she talking to?" I ask.

"I can't be giving out that kind of information," he says. "Are you two writing an article?"

Mike says, "Yes," while I say, "No," which makes the sheriff say, "Is there something going on that I should know about?"

Again Mike says, "Yes" and I say, "No."

Here's the thing. The biggest mistakes I made with the last sheriff was questioning his investigation skills, telling him what to investigate, and tearing apart his cases. I also blurted out too many details about crimes. Details I shouldn't be privy to unless I was involved, making me look suspicious. I am not about to make that mistake with the new sheriff.

Mike, on the other hand, he hasn't made my mistakes. Yet.

"Dude, the killer was sitting in her front seat eating ice cream, and that's what caused her to drive off the road."

Ah! We don't know that anyone was in Vanessa's car. That's a total guess on our part. I'm sending mental messages to Mike, telling him to shut up.

He's not getting them. "Don't you care that a twenty-year-old girl went missing six months ago?" Mike asks.

The sheriff has the most perplexed expression on his face it's almost comical. *Almost.*

"Do you not know about Lux Piefer?" Mike asks.

Oh, hell. I'm about to stuff Mike in a receptacle!

"Should I?" the sheriff asks.

"Vanessa was investigating the disappearance of Lux. She stopped by Fernn Valley on her way to San Francisco six months ago, when there was the book festival. She hasn't been seen or heard from since. Sheriff Vance knew about this but didn't do anything," Mike says.

"And you think this crash has to do with Lux's disappearance?"

Mike says, "Yes" and I say, "No."

Gah. We need to be on the same page.

Sheriff Executer runs a hand down his tired face. I can see his thoughts. He's exhausted and stressed and in over his head.

When he took the position as undersheriff, he never imagined that he'd have to step up and be the actual sheriff one day. He doesn't want to investigate car crashes or missing people or any crimes. All he wants to do is go fishing.

I completely understand how he feels.

Minus the fishing part.

"Vance never told me anything about anyone disappearing at the book festival," he finally says.

"Do you know where Sheriff Vance is?" I ask.

"He's in Las Vegas, licking his wounds, waiting for the scandal to die down before he returns."

"When was the last time someone talked to him?" Mike asks.

"Not since he took off." Sheriff hooks his thumbs into his belt loops. "I'll go through his old files when I get back to the station. Do you have any clue as to where this girl could have gone?"

"She was killed," Mike says. "We think Vanessa was either on the phone with the killer when she crashed, or the killer was—"

I ram my elbow into Mike's side to shut him up, since my mental messages aren't working. Again, we don't know anything for sure, and spitting out absolutes will only make Mike look suspicious.

"Murder is a big accusation." The sheriff adopts a serious tone. "How do you know these details, son?"

"Don't mind him." I pat Mike's arm. "We're mourning the loss of our friend. Car accidents are hard for him because ... *you know*. His mother and that whole story. It's been a rough couple of weeks. There have been a lot of uprooted feelings."

"What are you doing?" Vanessa hisses. "Why aren't you agreeing with Mike? This sheriff isn't shady. He could help us."

I give Mike a softer jab with my elbow, hoping he won't say anything more about Vanessa. Lucky for me, he does much better with physical messages than mental ones.

"Super hard." Mike wipes at his dry eyes.

I give him another little jab because there's no need to overdo the dramatics.

The sheriff's eyes go from Mike to me and back again. "If you two know something I should know, then I hope you'd let me know."

"I know." I nod. "We will. Just real ... quickly." I clear my throat. "Where are Vanessa's personal belongings?"

"They're with her at the coroner's office, but if you're telling me this is foul play, then I'm going to have to make sure we get those back."

Oh, geez. This is exactly why you don't talk to the authorities! We need that phone now.

"Uh ... uh ... did I say foul play?" Mike is backtracking. "I-I'm so sad. That's it. Sad and I am not making sense. Because I'm ... sad. That darn Vanessa. She was always on her phone. Right, Zoe?"

Here's the thing, I suck at lying on the spot. "For. Sure. That Vanessa. Darn. Her."

The sheriff massages his temples and mutters something under his breath.

"You two need to seriously work on your acting," Vanessa says with a shake of her head.

The sheriff has no idea what to make of us. Part of him wants to let us go and ignore what he's heard. The other part—the bigger part—feels he owes it to the people of Fernn Valley to make sure this was a car accident and nothing more. He's also concerned about Lux. He had no idea a young girl had gone missing.

Crap. I thought dealing with a shady sheriff was hard. Dealing with a sheriff who has a conscience is going to be more difficult.

"I'm crazy!" I blurt out. "Super crazy. I am seriously looney.

Like, I make stuff up all the time. Lots of stuff. I talk to myself. I see people. I—"

Mike jabs me with his elbow, and I snap my mouth closed. I may have overdone it.

"How about I take you home," the sheriff says, his face full of concern. "You're not well."

"No, I'm in charge of her today." Mike pats the top of my head. "Now, now, Zoe. See? This is just an accident. Nothing more. Let's get you home." He grabs my shoulders and maneuvers me away from the tree. "Is he buying it?" Mike mutters under his breath once our backs are turned.

I look over my shoulder. The sheriff puts his head in his hands. "Not sure," I whisper. "He's mostly wondering who would take over as sheriff if he were to quit today. Also, he wants to go fishing."

"Do you still feel the dark spirit?"

I concentrate. The dark spirit is here, and I check over my shoulder again. The sheriff is now talking to Mike's Uncle Gary, who is hooking the car up to the tow truck, while Elvin is still snapping pictures of the inside of the vehicle. Gary still has that grin plastered on his face, as if the site of the car is causing him great personal joy. I back up an inch, hoping to catch his feelings, when Mike pulls me forward.

"What are you doing?" I hiss.

"I told the sheriff I would take you home."

"I can't go home now."

"Obviously. But we have to get Vanessa's phone and laptop."

Vanessa is in our faces. "Can you two stop talking and start walking?"

Hold on. "What about Tanner and Gary and Elvin?"

"What about them?" Mike asks.

"I'm getting some negative vibes here. It's hard for me to tell from where I am standing whether the dark presence is coming from Elvin or Gary."

"My uncle Gary is about as shady as you can get. He has no problems breaking the law. Some say he's worse than my dad."

Yikes, that's pretty bad.

"So what do we know about Elvin?" I ask.

"Other than he sounds like Kermit the Frog, nothing," says Mike. "But if any of them had anything to do with Lux's disappearance, then they're going to want to get their hands on that phone before anyone else. And we have no idea where Tanner is."

Good point. "Let's go."

CHAPTER FIVE

We're back in the car, driving to the coroner's office. I glance at the clock every few seconds, watching the minutes tick by. This is so freaking stressful. My heart feels as if it's about to climb out of my chest and run for cover.

"What about the ice cream wrapper?" Mike asks from his spot in the back seat.

"I did see the ice cream truck this morning," says Vanessa. "There has to be some connection there."

"Who drives the ice cream truck?" I ask.

"Dominick Sanders," says Mike.

Aha. He's right. Here's what I know about Dominick Sanders: He's tall and dark and has nicely groomed eyebrows. He's Mr. Sanders' son from his first marriage, works at the Food Mart, and he drives the ice cream truck.

"The ice cream truck was at the book festival," I say. "I remember it being there, and I saw it in Tanner's thoughts. Is it possible that he killed Lux, knew you were in town looking for her, saw you driving away from Brian's house, jumped in your car, and ... I'm not sure what could have happened next."

Vanessa taps her chin. "He could have jumped in my car to tell me he knows who killed Lux."

"Dude, Dominick Sanders can knock the ball out of the park every time," Mike adds, for no apparent reason. "Probably the best swing on the team."

Vanessa turns around to face him, even if he can't see her. "That literally has nothing to do with anything."

"Not so fast," I say, keeping my eyes on the road. "Dominick is on the softball team with Tanner. Are the two friends?"

"We're a team," he says, as if that explains everything.

I don't play sports. But I have read many sports romance novels, and it seems like teammates stick together. "If anything, Dominick likely sold that fudge pop to whoever ate it this morning. He could have answers."

What I need to do is talk to Dominick face-to-face so I can see his thoughts. In the meantime, hopefully we can get her phone and see whom she was talking to.

I'm not sure how we'll get Vanessa's phone, being that we're not family. The good news is we have a spirit who can float through walls and is determined to find answers.

I glance up into the rearview mirror at Mike. "Has the future changed?"

"Yeah. I'm going to barf."

I chuckle. Wait. "For reals?"

He sucks in a breath, looking green. "Can you go easy on the brakes, *please*?"

"Of course." I return my focus to the road and slam on the brakes. Mike hits the back of the seat, and Vanessa yelps. There's a deer staring at us.

"You okay back there, Mike? Uh ... Mike?" I turn around. "Yikes."

So it turns out that both Vanessa and Mike are prone to car sickness. Since I'm not, it's best if I take the back seat. I'm short, so it's not terribly uncomfortable. Mike could not look happier behind the wheel—even if I do make him obey the speed limit.

The coroner's office is located next to the sheriff station on the west end of town. It's a pale building with an American flag proudly displayed out front. The doors automatically open as we approach. I can feel the presence of multiple spirits here but none that have a need to show themselves. A relief. I'm not ready to handle more than one spirit at a time.

A twenty-something-year-old man with a uniform on and wavy black hair that falls to his shoulders is sitting behind a desk, playing solitaire.

"Dude, Yutchson." Mike raises his hand up in the air.

"Bro!" Yutchson stands, and the two do that half-hug/half-handclasp thing guys do.

"I didn't know you worked here," Mike says. "This is Zoe Lane. Zoe, this is Zeke. The second best outfielder on the softball team."

"Second best? Man, get out of here." Zeke gives Mike a playful shove. "You wish you had my skills."

"He's pretty handy to have around," Vanessa says. "He seems to know everyone."

Yes, he does.

"Nice to meet you, Zeke," I say.

"You, too. I've heard some seriously ca-razy tales about you, girl."

Great.

"I'm going to look for me," Vanessa announces and walks through a wall.

"Dude, so glad you work here." Mike has a friendly hand on Zeke's shoulder. "Help us out. Fatal car crash this morning. They brought the body in. We need some deets."

Deets?

"Bro, I wish I could help you out."

"Dude, totally off the record. I won't say anything. Just want to know if her next of kin have been notified, when they'll be here, and if we can get her stuff."

Vanessa jumps through the wall. "I found me," she announces then whips around and disappears again.

Mike and I share a look. I know he heard her, but I'm not sure if he caught the excitement in her tone. She must have found information. No one is that happy to see themselves dead.

"Bro, you know I got nothing but mad love for you." Zeke puts a hand over his heart. "I can't risk losing my job, bro."

"I'd never want that, man," Mike says. "Whatever you got is between you and me and Zoe here. You can trust her."

Zeke relents then takes a seat behind his desk. He scoots his chair closer and wiggles the mouse around. "Are you talking about Vanessa Tobin? Wait, isn't that Windsor's girl?"

"Ex-girl," I say. "And, yes."

"Oh, man. I hate to hear that. Terrible. Bro, they bring all the bodies in through the back. All I know is what I see on the computer here. Looks like she hasn't been here that long. They haven't even notified the next of kin. Does Windsor know?"

"We're not sure," I say. "Would he be able to get her belongings?"

"If the family gives him permission."

Vanessa reappears. "I think my stuff is in a bag under the gurney I'm on. I can't get it."

"You're saying that her boyfriend can get her personal belongings with permission from her family?" I confirm with Zeke so Vanessa can hear.

"I do not have a boyfriend," she says indignantly. "My boyfriend cut all ties when he fell for some wide-eyed home wrecker at work!"

Wait ... whaaaa? I've lost the ability to speak.

So has Mike. Who is standing there with his mouth wide open.

Zeke pokes Mike with the end of his pen. "You cool, bro?"

"I'm ... *cool.*" His eyes slide to meet mine. I know what he's thinking without having to read his thoughts.

Backfire. Backfire. Backfire.

"So ... um ... if we have permission from her family, we can get ahold of Vanessa's things?" I ask Zeke, trying and failing to keep my voice from shaking.

"The only person they'd contact is my father," Vanessa says. "He lives in Brookings, Oregon. That's not too far from here. Ask to speak to the coroner. Maybe we can talk him into handing over my stuff. At the very least we need my cell."

"Zeke," I say. "Can we talk to the coroner working on Vanessa?"

"Let me check." Zeke grabs the phone on his desk and dials an extension.

Mike and I take the opportunity to congregate in the corner, near a ficus plant, so we can talk to Vanessa.

"What did you see back there?" I ask.

Vanessa grits her teeth. "I'm on the exam table. My face has a few scrapes. Nothing around my neck that would suggest being strangled. No bullet holes or knife wounds that I could see. I'm pretty sure I died because I drove off the road."

It must be horrible to examine your own dead body, but Vanessa is not fazed. She's in work mode.

Mike steps closer, accidentally going *through* Vanessa.

"Whoa! Watch where you're going there, buddy," she says.

Mike looks at me, a giant question mark etched on his face.

"You walked through Vanessa."

"Oh, my bad." He takes a step back and goes *through* Vanessa again.

"Stay still!" Vanessa's face is pressed up against Mike's. "Stop moving."

Mike plasters his arms to his side like a toy solider. "What I was going to say is that we should tell Sheriff Executor everything we know. We're running out of time, and the more people we have working on this the better. He can find out who Vanessa last talked to more easily than we can."

Vanessa gives a dismissive wave of her hand. "Zoe is right. We need to keep this between us. No one will believe that you guys can hear me, and if you go running your mouths, you're only going to look suspicious." She lets out a short laugh. "After Zoe's 'I'm crazy' spiel, there's no way the sheriff will take anything you say seriously."

She's right.

"Did you see anything else back there?" I ask Vanessa.

Her expression morphs into a frown. "No. It sucks that I can't use my hands. I would have grabbed my stuff."

"Think hard," I say. "Try and remember who you were talking to on the phone."

Vanessa squeezes her eyes shut. "I was in my car. I saw the ice cream truck." She lifts her lids and shrugs. "Then I was at your house."

Mike checks over his shoulder. Zeke is still on the phone. "It's crazy annoying that the dead can't remember how they died."

"Annoying to us only," I say. "The deceased shouldn't have to relive the horror of their death."

Vanessa is shaking her head. "It's annoying to the dead as well. Hey. Your guy is off the phone."

Both Mike and I shuffle back to Zeke's desk.

"Good news and bad news," he says. "The good news is that he's willing to speak to you. The bad news is he said you'd have to wait until tomorrow. He wants to gather as much information as possible before he talks to the press."

Dang it.

"He did say he'd rush for a price," Zeke adds.

A price? He can't be serious.

"How much?" Vanessa asks.

"How much?" I repeat in horror. She can't possibly think we'd pay a coroner to give us sensitive information.

"Not sure," answers Zeke. "Ten should probably do it. He didn't give me a number."

"Ten?" Mike chokes out. "Like thousand?"

"Not bad," Vanessa says. "I know journalists who have paid more."

I gawk at her.

"What?" she says defensively. "You cross gray lines for vital information."

Sure, but ten thousand dollars is about nine thousand nine hundred and ninety-eight dollars more than I currently have.

Mike pulls me aside. "I do have the money my aunt left me."

"I am not letting you spend that money," I whisper, then spin around. "You can tell the coroner that exchanging money for information is illegal." I make a massive U-turn and storm out of the building.

"You don't need to get all high and mighty," Vanessa says once we're outside. "We could pay him for my stuff. Or at the very least, pay him so we can look at my stuff. Now we don't have any of my stuff. I want my stuff!"

"We're not breaking the law." I use my fob to unlock my car and open the doors. "And I'm not high and mighty. We're going to Brian's. He's the closest thing to next of kin we have right now, and he could help us get your *stuff*." Also, I want to read his thoughts so I can find out who was in the body bag. "Here." I toss the keys to Mike. "Drive carefully."

CHAPTER SIX

Brian lives at the end of a dirt road in a farm-style home with blue shutters, tan exterior, and white trim. The grass is mowed into straight lines, and the bushes are manicured into circles. It's quite charming.

"Good. His car is here." Vanessa points to his silver sedan parked in the driveway.

"What's the plan?" Mike asks.

Not sure. I do not want to talk to Brian in front of Vanessa. Maybe I should just come clean now and tell her that I am the home wrecker from work that Brian fell for. But the time to come clean was when we first met. Now she'll feel betrayed. *Ugh.* Why, oh why didn't I just come clean when we were at my house? Why? Why? Why?

"What are you doing with your face?" Vanessa asks. "Are you sick? We don't have time for you to get sick. Mind over matter!"

"No. I'm just ... thinking. That's all."

Mike parks in the driveway behind Brian's car because a *baby like this shouldn't be on dirt.* The baby he's referring to is my car.

"What now?" He turns around in his seat to face me.

"How about I go talk to him and you two stay here?"

"No. We all go." Vanessa disappears and reappears outside. She smooths down her hair and looks at her wrist. She misses her tattoo. I'm not sure where it went.

After we die, we're returned to our prime age. Vanessa was only twenty-five when she *...oh*. Vanessa's spirit must be younger. She did say she'd just gotten it a few weeks ago. The good news is she won't need her tattoo to remember her grandma by. She'll be with her soon.

The three of us walk up the driveway, side by side.

"I think we should tell him the truth," Mike says. "He'll know Vanessa is with us, and he can help us find out what happened. There are so many rumors about you seeing ghosts that he has to have a hunch it's true."

"No, he doesn't," Vanessa says. "We talked about it a few weeks ago. We were in bed, and I asked if he'd heard the rumors about you. He said he had and that they weren't true. He said you were quirky but that people who claim to speak to the dead are nothing but frauds."

Ouch.

"That was before he started falling for the woman at work," she adds.

Ugh. Right. That. "Uh ..." I clear my throat. "How do you know there was another woman?"

"A hunch," she says. "He started pulling back and working late. He claimed to have been in an accident that totaled his car, but there wasn't a scratch on him. I think she was responsible for his car, and he was covering for her."

That's pretty much exactly how it happened. Dang it. I need to tell Vanessa I'm the other woman.

"Dude, I have a good idea," Mike says. "Vanessa and I will go around the back and see if there's anything suspicious."

Vanessa scrunches her face. "What are you talking about?"

"I ... uh ... Zoe said Brian is hiding a body bag. It might be in the backyard."

Vanessa cocks her thumb to Mike. "Is this guy serious?"

Yes, he is. He wants to distract Vanessa so Brian and I can be alone. I appreciate the gesture, but I can't do this anymore. Lying to Vanessa is the opposite of what a medium should do. I have a responsibility to protect her.

"Vanessa, we need to talk—"

"No time for talking." Mike cuts me off and taps his wrist, as if pointing to a watch. "Times a-ticking. People are a-dying."

"But—" I start to protest.

"No time." Mike waves for Vanessa to follow and takes off towards the side of the house.

"I seriously doubt there's a body bog in the backyard. But whatever. You're the mediums." Vanessa throws her arms up in the air and follows.

I really want to tell Vanessa the truth, but Mike is right. We're running out of time, and I suspect the conversation about Brian and me will be a long one.

I knock on the door and fidget with my hands. Brian answers holding a paper plate with a slice of pizza. There's a strand of dark hair dangling on his forehead, and he's wearing a blue T-shirt and khaki shorts. I've never seen him so casual before. This is certainly not a man in a state of mourning ... crap. He doesn't know! Or he doesn't care enough to think about his dead ex-girlfriend. Either way, Vanessa is not on his mind. Rather, he's feeling foolish for kissing me. Being that he's my boss, he's concerned I'll sue.

"Zoe, I'm glad you came." Brian opens the door wider, about to invite me in, then thinks better of it. We shouldn't be alone behind closed doors. That's what the article on sexual harassment in the workplace that he read after I sent him away this morning told him. "Zoe, I owe you an apology. I misread our relationship, and I hope that you'll still work at *The Gazette*. I can promise you that I'll never make a pass at you again."

"Never?" I squeak out. "I-I, no, you didn't misread anything. It's only that right now is not a good time."

"I didn't know you were in a relationship with Mike."

Vanessa reappears and takes me by surprise.

Uh ...

"What are you talking about?" Vanessa asks.

I plaster a smile of my face.

"He's seriously eating pizza after he finds out I'm dead? What a guy."

"Brian." I blow out a breath in an attempt to calm my frazzled nerves. "Have you talked to Sheriff Executer?"

"No, not recently. Why?"

Vanessa's hand flies to her mouth. "He doesn't know yet."

I shake my head slightly. He's completely clueless. Fernn Valley is small, word travels fast, and I know he won't remain in the dark for long. I need to work fast.

"I want to know what happened at a shore. You need to come clean, Brian. What happened?" I don't mention the body bag. Not yet. The hope is to get him talking about the shore, and whoever is in the bag will be revealed through his thoughts.

"*O-kay*," he says, but his eyes betray his reluctance. "How much do you already know?" "

I furrow my brow and concentrate on his feelings. He's currently drowning in remorse and angst. He's thinking about a shore ... an offshore ... an offshore account ... "An offshore account!" I say victoriously. Until I remember there is nothing to be victorious about. At least the whole *shore* thing makes sense now.

Brain straightened to full height. "Who told you?"

"It's not important," I say. "What is important is that you tell me the truth."

He turns his face away and examines the doorframe, too ashamed to make eye contact. "I worked for Vanessa's dad during my last semester of college."

Vanessa is shaking her head. "No. No. I don't like where this is going."

Me, neither.

"He's a trust attorney with a lot of clients who love him. Most of them are older and too trusting. I noticed accounts were off-balance. Money was missing. Not enough to raise red flags. Just enough to go unnoticed."

"My dad would not take money from his clients," Vanessa says, red in the cheeks. "He would not. I cannot believe Brian is making up these lies! If that's the truth, why wouldn't he have told me?"

"I couldn't tell Vanessa," says Brian as if answering Vanessa's question. "She'd accuse me of lying. So I ..." He sucks in his bottom lip, attempting to regain his composure. "I told her grandma what was going on."

"You did what!" Vanessa explodes. "You told my grandma!"

"Oh, my gosh." I slap a hand over my mouth. "Brian ..." The body bag! The body bag belonged to Vanessa's grandma. "She died after you told her?"

Brian nods his head slightly but offers no words.

"I don't like this," Vanessa is trembling all over. "I don't like this at all. Stop! Make him stop, Zoe. My dad would never hurt anyone!"

"She confronted him," says Brian. "That's not why I told her. I'd hoped she'd have a reasonable explanation as to why there was missing money. I'd hoped she'd tell me there was nothing to worry about. I had no idea she'd been harboring resentment towards Max for the last twenty years. I had no idea she thought

Max was emotionally abusive, and that's why Vanessa's mother left. I had no idea she was anything but a sweet old lady who liked to bake and knit. When I told her, it was like someone ignited a fire inside of her. She did more digging and found out the money was sent to an offshore account. When she told me, I urged her to call the police. The next morning, she was found dead in her home after a supposed break-in."

"My dad wouldn't kill my grandma!"

"I suspect that she confronted him, and he took care of her. She knew too much," he says.

"Brian," I say, feeling a bit light-headed. "Why didn't you tell the police?"

"Because Vanessa would have never forgiven me for turning in her father. Even if he was in the wrong. And I worried she'd try to protect him and get herself caught up in something illegal."

"He's right," she says. "He's absolutely right. But now I will never forgive him for telling my grandma!"

I'm starting to put the pieces together. "That's why you left Portland," I say to Brian. "You wanted to put distance between you and Vanessa, and between you and Vanessa's dad."

Wait, I suddenly remember our conversation at the coroner's office. "I thought he lived closer than Portland?"

"He moved and retired after Vanessa's grandma died," says Brian.

"Does he know you know?" I ask.

"If he did, I suspect that I wouldn't still be alive. But I thought you knew all this already?"

"Uh ... I did. Mostly."

Vanessa sits down and drops her head into her hands. She's desperately trying to shove her feelings into a receptacle.

The phone rings from inside the house, and Brian excuses himself.

I crouch down beside Vanessa. "I'm so sorry."

"This can't be true. It can't be true at all." She's tracing an infinity symbol on her wrist. "I don't want this to be true."

"I don't either. But I know Brian is telling the truth."

"I know he is, too. Everything makes so much more sense now. That's why he's been pulling away. Not because he doesn't love me, and not because he's fallen for a girl at work. He was just trying to protect me."

Mike peeks around the side of the house, and I frantically signal for him to stay hidden by making an X with my arms. I need a minute alone with Vanessa.

Before I can get the words out, there's a loud crash. Brian! I step over the pizza slice on the floor and rush inside. Brian has a death grip on the kitchen counter, his chest rising and falling in rapid motions, and a vase is shattered at his feet.

He knows.

He's unable to fully process the information, too weighted by shock. But he knows. That was Mrs. Muffin calling, wanting to see if she could stop by and drop off cookies for him. She didn't know that he didn't know. Now he does. She told him everything. She's the one who made the 911 call.

"Brian," I reach for his arm, and he yanks back.

He meets my gaze and sucks in a breath. "You knew."

"I did but—"

"You knew when I was at your house. You never mentioned the Lux case until today. And you never talked about Vanessa. You two don't know each other. There's no way. You tricked me into telling you about her-her-her father ..." His mind is moving father than his mouth can. "Who are you working for?"

"What? No one!"

Brian looks past me and narrows his eyes. I spin around, and there's Mike standing in the doorway, even though I'd specifically told him to stay put. Honestly!

"You!" Brian eyes are so big I swear they're about to fall out of his face. "You!"

Mike holds up his palms. "I'm sorry, man."

Vanessa is still sitting on the porch, seemingly unaware that her ex-boyfriend looks like he's about to kill one of her mediums.

"Let's calm down and talk about this," I say. "There's a lot more to this story. Brian, there's something I need to tell you."

"You did it!"

I take a step back. "Huh?"

"You two." He's looking at Mike and me. "How would you have known she was dead? When I was at your house, she wasn't even dead yet. Mrs. Muffin said the accident happened *at* eleven. I got to your house *at* eleven. There's no way you could have known she was dead, unless you didn't know she was dead, but you knew she was going to die."

Oh, hell. "Brian, there's a reason that I knew, and it isn't what you're thinking."

"Dude," Mike takes a cautious step forward. "You have to hear us out."

"You two were in on it together." I've never seen Brian so upset before. His eyes are wild, his cheeks are red, and his glasses are fogged. He's no Mr. Rodgers right now. That's for sure.

"I was at Zoe's house the entire time you were there," Mike says.

"I didn't see your car," Brian retorts.

"It was parked across the street. It's *still* parked across the street."

I actually didn't know that.

"What about your uncles?" Brian asks Mike.

Mike shakes his head. "What about them?"

"Vanessa tried to question both your dad and uncles about Lux Piefer, and they all chased her away."

"Dude, we both know my family isn't exactly on the straight and narrow," Mike says.

Brian tilts his head. "Are you?"

"Brian!" I say. "I know you're upset right now, but Mike didn't do anything."

He's not buying it and turns his attention to me. "Are you working for Max?"

"No!"

"Vanessa's death wasn't an accident." Brian yanks open a kitchen drawer and removes his keys and wallet. "Just like her grandma didn't die in an armed robbery."

"Brian, no. You have this all wrong." I'm following him out the door. He passes Vanessa and marches to his car. "Where are you going?"

"To find out what happened."

"Wait, Brian. Listen to me. You're not going to figure this out."

"Yes, I will." He flings open his car door with so much force I fear it's going to come off the hinges. "To think that I actually broke up with Vanessa to be with you. And you were using me to get information for Max!"

Brian gets in his car and backs out of the driveway, his tires screeching.

Mike and I chase after him, but he's not slowing down. He throws the car into drive and peels down the road, leaving a cloud of dirt behind him. "I'm a medium!" I scream. "I can see Vanessa!"

There's no use. He's already down the street.

I'm hunched over with my hands on my knees, attempting to catch my breath.

"Well, that escalated quickly," Mike says, gasping for air. "We went from thinking he was a criminal to him thinking we are."

"He dumped me for you!" Vanessa appears in front of us in the middle of the street. "You lied to me." She looks so incandescent that I start backing up.

"This isn't what you think."

"I'm such an idiot." She gives a short, mocking-type laugh. "I didn't see it because I was concerned about being dead. Brian was at your house this morning because he had officially cut all ties with me. I can't believe I didn't see it before!"

Vanessa suddenly rushes at me, and I fall to the ground. "I promise you, nothing ever happened between us until this morning when he showed up at my house."

Mike looks totally freaked out. If only he could see Vanessa standing over me. Then he'd really have something to freak out about.

"We've only kissed once, and that happened this morning," I say then flinch, expecting a blow. "Then you showed up, and I sent him away."

"You lied to me."

My words are all jumbled up in my mouth. I don't even know what to say, except, "I'm sorry."

"Sorry that my medium lied to me?" She rushes me again, and I fall back on my hands. Vanessa is scary when she's angry. I sure wish she'd stuff these feeling in a capsule.

"Stop it!" Mike yells loud enough for the neighbors to step out onto their porches to see what is going on. "It's changed!"

"What has?" Vanessa gets in his face. "What has changed?"

Mike's eyes go distant. "The future. It's changed. The vision has changed ... It's not good. It's really, really not good." He's shaking all over, and I rise to my feet and take his face in my hands.

Oh, my. I can ... see what he's seeing. *Almost.*

Mike wraps me in his arms and hugs me so tightly I lose my breath, his body still trembling. I wiggle free and rise to my toes.

I lower Mike's face so our foreheads are touching, and I close my eyes, concentrating on our emotional connection.

For the first time I can see his vision. It's almost as if I'm looking through a foggy window. There's a forest filled with pine trees. It's dark. Not the pitch black of midnight. More so the early hours of the evening. I'm wearing the same gray sweat suit, my knees covered in mud. Mike is there. He's wearing a black shirt with a clown on the front, and his nose is bleeding. A woman that looks vaguely familiar takes a protective stance in front of me. She looks a lot like an older version of the Lux I saw in Tanner's thoughts. This could be Jolene! The woman takes a protective stance in front of me. Mike takes a protective stance in front of her. I can't see Vanessa, but I sense that she's there. There are gunshots and explosions in the background. A tall man pushes through the bushes. His face and hands are covered in mud. I don't think I recognize him. It's hard to know for sure through the fog. He holds up a gun and aims it at Mike's chest. I try to push past Jolene when Brian jumps out from behind a bush. I scream and tell him to leave. A shot is fired, and Brian falls to the ground.

CHAPTER SEVEN

I can't quite move. My forehead is still pressed against Mike's. Of course I didn't want anyone to die, but I *really* don't want Brian to die! I fall back and place my hands on my knees, feeling sick. "Can everyone just stay alive for five freaking minutes," I cry out in distress.

Vanessa is fluttering around. "Tell me what happened. Now!"

"The future has changed." Mike's voice sounds strangled and far away. "Now ... Brian dies."

I can almost see the anger draining from Vanessa. "H-how does he die?"

"He's shot," I say.

"Then we have to stop him!" she bellows directly into my eardrum. "Call him!"

I fumble my phone out of my pocket and call Brian. "It goes straight to voicemail," I say in a panic. "Brian. Please, call me. I can see Vanessa. She's here with me. Call me back!" I hang up and send a text with the same message. "Where do you think he went?" I ask Vanessa.

"I have no idea." Vanessa is stricken and starts pacing.

"Also, I think it's Jolene who is there with us," I say. "That's who is going to take the bullet for me."

"How the hell does Jolene get from Portland to Fernn Valley so fast?" Vanessa asks.

"She must already be on her way," I say. "What's her number?"

Vanessa's face goes blank. "I don't know anyone's number!"

"Okay, what's her email address?"

"I don't know anyone's email address! This is why we need my freaking phone!"

Mike shakes his head, as if waking from a daydream. "Dude, you think that's Jolene with us?"

"I'm almost positive," I say.

"We need to split up." Vanessa is oozing determination. "New plan. Step one: Mike, call *all* your softball buddies, and tell everyone to look for Brian. We have to find Brian. That is now priority one. Step two: tell all your friends to find Tanner. We've completely lost sight of Tanner. We need to find Tanner. Even though I can't feel other's feelings, I could tell he's hiding information. Step one for Zoe and me: we will talk to the Ishmaels about the boarding. Zoe can read their thoughts, and we'll figure out if she was there, and if Tanner was there, and who else might be involved. Step three for Mike: get the money your aunt left you. Take it *all* out. Or as much as they'll let you. We need cash in case we need to bribe. Step two for Zoe and me: we talk to Dominick, and Zoe can read his thoughts. Who did he sell a fudge pop to this morning? Did he see anything? Did he kill Lux? We need to talk to him before word gets out that we're looking for him. If he's got something to hide, he'll run. Step four for Mike: I need to find more information on how Sheriff Vance handled the investigation. The police reports I have are minimal at best. It says he verified that the hotel was booked that night. That's it. We need to find out where he is, how long he has been there, and if he really did look into Lux's case at all ... Are you texting Brian or writing down my steps?"

I look up from my phone. "Texting Brian, and my mom, and dad, and Mrs. Batch, and every number that I have. We need to find Brian."

"Good. Step three for Zoe and me: we get my phone. I don't care if we have to bribe, steal, or cross lines. If we can see who I was talking to, it could give a clue as to who killed Lux. Do you all understand me?"

"Yes," Mike says, his phone out. "I'm already sending out a group text right now."

"What about Jolene?" I ask. "How are we supposed to reach her?"

"Jolene is a tough cookie. If she'll be in Fernn Valley tonight, then she's already on her way. There's nothing we can do. She doesn't die. So let's not concentrate on her right now."

"Are you sure?"

"Positive."

Okay. Okay. Okay. "Splitting up is good." I rub my chest. It's possible that I'm having a mild heart attack. "We can't be together in the forest if we make a conscious effort to not be together at all. Except ..." I massage my temples, willing my brain to work better. "Shouldn't we put forth all our efforts into finding Brian? We can sit him down, tell him everything, and make sure he doesn't go in the forest."

"He will not stop until he finds answers. I know him. He's not going to listen to you about ghosts and visions. Not in his current state of mind." Vanessa focuses on me. "I will forgive you for kissing my boyfriend if you keep him alive."

"But—" I start to protest, and she cuts me off.

"No more *buts*. No more *I can't*. No more *ummmmmm*. No more second-guessing yourself. You are the most incredibly talented woman I have ever met. And that's saying a lot coming from me, because I currently hate you," Vanessa says, and she means it. I can feel it. "What I need from you right now is to keep Brian alive. Got it? I don't care about anything else. He needs to live."

I nod my head.

"Now, let's go catch a killer. Everyone in." Vanessa puts her hand out, and I hoover my hand above hers.

"We're doing a cheer," I say to Mike, and he places his hand on top of mine. His skin is ice cold, which, oddly enough, warms my heart and brings a sense of comfort to this high-stress situation.

"Go for it." Vanessa is staring at me expectantly. "Empower us."

Oh. Empower. *Err* ... I lick my lips and frantically search through my memory bank. I've read the entire Sexy Coaches from the South series. They gave exceptional motivational speeches right before games ... and before they whisked their lovers to the showers. But whatever. Think. Think. *Think*.

Okay.

Got it.

"Play hard. Fight hard. Be hard."

Vanessa and Mike stare at me with their mouths open.

Errr ... "Talent without hard work is nothing," I add.

"Okay." Vanessa nods. "We can do something with ... that. Anyway." She lifts her hand up in the air. I do the same. Then Mike follows. I can feel that Vanessa is trying her hardest to cheer us on, hoping that we'll come through for her.

I sure hope we don't let her down.

The three of us do a collective sigh, then pile into my car. I drive this time, and we drop Mike off at my house. He has his red Jeep parked down the street.

I check my watch. We have roughly five hours until sundown. Which is not a lot of time to stop a murder.

Before we take off, I dig around in my bag and pull out a notepad and a pen, which is silver and engraved with my last name, a present from my dad on my first day of work.

"There is no time for doodling," Vanessa says.

"I'm not doodling. There are too many moving parts, and I like to write everything down to make sense of what information we have, what information we need, and who our suspects are." I click my pen and find a fresh sheet of paper. "We think that Jolene was supposed to die today, but instead you did. Which means somehow the perp was going to kill Jolene, but something happened, and they changed their mind last minute and killed you instead."

"You're left-handed," Vanessa says.

"Yes."

"Me, too."

We share a second of camaraderie then continue.

"We know that you drove past an ice cream truck and that eventually you ended up near the *Welcome to Fernn Valley* sign." I add this to my *Things We Know* column.

"There's the fudge pop wrapper."

"Right. We have zero idea how that ended up there or its relevance, but it does tie back to the ice cream truck." I write this down. "We really need to talk to Dominick. Tanner knows something about Lux. He could very well be our guy. Then there's Gary, Mike's uncle. He has a dark spirit. We don't know if the spirit is dark because he's a Handhoff or because he did something to Lux. Then there's Sheriff Vance, we don't have much evidence on him aside from the fact that he originally worked the case and he's a creepy person."

"What about Elvin?" Vanessa asks. "You asked about him at the crash site."

"You're right. Honestly, I really just need to get into all these men's heads, and fast."

"We've got this. Together we are greater than any obstacle that stands in our way."

"You should probably do the motivational talks from now on." I start the car.

"Probably. Now, go!"

The dry cleaner isn't busy, and when we step inside, Mrs. Ishmael is sitting in a chair next to the sewing machine, crying and shaking her head. Much to my surprise, Tanner is at her side, holding a box of tissue for his mother. Mrs. Ishmael grabs two, blows her nose, tosses them on the floor, and grabs two more.

"What a break!" Vanessa does a fist pump. "Yes! He's here. He's here. He's ... running."

What?

The little bells on the door jingle, and Tanner is halfway down the street.

Gah! I swear that boy is getting on my nerves!

I chase after him, dodging around people, jumping over plants, and I cut across the street (looking both ways first) and to the park. He's fast but winded. I'm slow but determined. I'm trying that whole *breathing, putting the pain inside a capsule* thing that Vanessa said to do, and it works!

Tanner reaches the duck pond and slips on the sand. For lack of a better idea, I lunge forward and pin him to the ground. I roll up and sit on his stomach, straddling him. He's huffing and puffing. I'm huffing and puffing. We huff and puff for a while.

... Still huffing ...

... Still puffing ...

Okay. Now I can talk. "What in the hell is wrong with you!?"

Tanner makes an *X* with his arms. He thinks this will stop me from reading his mind. He'd looked it up on the Internet after he escaped the first time.

"That doesn't work." I slap his arms away from his face. "Tell me what you know about Lux."

Vanessa is standing over us, cheering me on.

"I know her mom was here looking for her," Tanner wheezes out, and I sit up a little so he can breathe better. "That's it."

"We both know that's not the truth, Tanner. Save me the trouble and just fess up. Did you hurt her?"

"No! I didn't. I just ..." He's struggling to catch his breath.

"Stop," I say and concentrate on his thoughts. The image of Lux comes into my mind. But she's not at a book festival. She's hauling a suitcase down a long dark hallway, following Mrs. Ishmael. Tanner offers to help with her luggage, and she brushes him off. Lux enters the room, closes the door, and locks it. There's a jumble of thoughts coming from Tanner, mostly insecurities. He wonders why girls never give him the time of day. The next thought is of the early morning. Tanner walks down the same long dark hall and hears a scratching sound. He peeks into the room Lux was staying in, and there's Mr. Ishmael on all fours, scrubbing a red stain on the floor.

"What did you see!" Vanessa demands.

"Blood. I saw blood. I mean ... he saw blood. He's innocent, but he's worried his dad isn't." I scramble to get off of Tanner and rise to my feet. "By the way, women might be more apt to reciprocate your advances if you didn't wear shirts with saying like *Duct Tape Can't Fix Stupid, But it Can Muffle the Sound.* It makes you look creepy."

Tanner nods his head, struggling to catch his breath.

Good. Now back to the Ishmaels. I cut across the street (looking both ways), zigzag around people, jump over plants, and push open the door of the dry cleaners.

Mrs. Ishmael is still crying.

"Geez. Who died?" Vanessa asks.

I put my finger on the Bluetooth I'd shoved in my ear earlier. A prop I use when talking to the dead. Glad it hadn't fallen out during my chase. "You did ... oh, no." Mrs. Ishmael is not crying over Vanessa. She's upset about her cat. She learned the truth. Mrs. Batch told her. Great! Just freaking great. Not that I don't feel bad for Mrs. Ishmael. I can feel her anguish. But I really need information from her mind, and I'm less likely to get it if she's in a state of mourning.

Mrs. Ishmael grabs two tissues and continues to cry. "Did you hear about my cat?"

"Yes, I did hear," I say. "He died last year, right?"

"Yes, but we didn't know who had run him over. They just left him dead on the ground, and I never had a chance to say goodbye."

"I know this won't make sense right now, but you need to talk to Mike Handhoff. He can help you find closure."

"I don't want closure. I want justice. Whiskers was my very best friend. I loved him more than anyone else on this planet," she says, and she means it. I suddenly feel very bad for her son and her husband. Speaking of which ...

"Where is Mr. Ishmael?"

"At the pharmacy."

Oh, no. Mr. Sanders, who ran over the cat, *owns* the pharmacy, and Mr. Ishmael could be a murderer. Yikes!

I'm out the door again.

"Where are we going?" Vanessa follows me.

"Mr. Sanders, the town's pharmacist, is the one who ran over the cat."

The pharmacy is next door. It's also empty, except for Mr. Ishmael, who is yelling at Mr. Sanders over the counter. "We put up posters all over town, trying to find out who ran over the cat."

"The thing darted out in front of me! What was I supposed to do? Swerve and die myself?"

"Yes!"

"If the cat meant that much to you, then you should have kept him inside," Mr. Sanders says.

I grab ahold of Mr. Ishmael before he jumps over the counter. Yes, he could potentially be dangerous. But I know, thanks to Mike, that no one attempts to kill me until later. "Please calm down," I say.

"Why don't you come talk to me face-to-face like a man," Mr. Ishmael struggles to break free from the death grip I have on the back of his shirt.

"Maybe I will." Mr. Sanders pushes through a little swinging door out to the lobby.

Oh, geez.

I let go of Mr. Ishmael and position myself between the two men. "Stop!" I scream at the top of my lungs. "Stop it right now! People are dying!"

"No, cats are," Mr. Ishmael says and leaps forward.

I push him back. I am a small person, but I'm pumped full of adrenaline. I do not have time to deal with two grown men getting into a fistfight. Not right now.

The only problem is, I'm not pumped with enough adrenaline to keep the two men apart. I'm about to be sandwiched between the pharmacist and the dry cleaner. Not a fun place to be.

Just then, Mr. Ishmael falls to the ground and clutches his chest.

Oh, for heaven's sake. Why is everyone trying to die!

"Can't you wait until I'm done with you?" I kneel beside him and check his pulse. It's beating rapidly. I think it's a heart attack, until I gaze up at Vanessa.

"Now, act like an adult, dammit," she says. "We don't have time to deal with your hissy fits."

"What did you do?" I ask.

"I slapped him."

She *slapped* him?

"Don't go and have a heart attack on me." Mr. Sanders rolls Mr. Ishmael to his back. He looks terrible. His forehead is drenched, his cheeks are blanched, and his breathing is labored.

Vanessa looks at her hands then at the men. Before I can stop her, she slaps Mr. Sanders on the back with all her might. He lets out a yelp and falls forward.

Uhhhhh ...

I have never been around a spirit who can give heart attacks!

Mr. Sanders holds his arm and rolls to his side. "I felt a stab of cold."

Oh, phew. Not a heart attack.

The men sit up slowly. "What was that?" they ask each other.

"Are you okay?" I extend my hands to the two men. They grab hold and I fall down because—yep—still don't have the physical power to manhandle two giant, middle-aged men.

The three of us stand on our own.

Mr. Sanders uses the counter for support. "I'm sorry," he says, shaking his head. "I should have told you. I knew how much the cat meant to you, but he ran out in front of me, and I couldn't stop fast enough."

Mr. Ishmael is still rubbing his chest and sweating quite profusely. "I understand," he says, but he doesn't mean it. He's just trying really hard not to keel over.

It's the perfect time for me to intervene. "I have a question about a girl who stayed at your house six months ago, the day of the book festival." There's no time to beat around the bush, not with Brian's life on the line. "Your son saw you scrubbing blood off the floor the day after a twenty-year-old girl named Lux Piefer checked in. She hasn't been heard or seen since. Did you kill her?"

Vanessa nods in approval. "Assertive. I like it."

Mr. Ishmael dramatically throws his arms in the air, as if someone just came up behind him and yelled, *Boo!* "What the Sam Hill are you talking about, woman? Well, I never ... I never! I never. Never. Never. Never."

"Okay. Okay. Okay. Got it. You never what?"

"I never killed anyone. Don't you go spreading rumors. It's bad for business."

"Why were you cleaning up blood on the floor the morning after Lux checked in"?"

"Because there was blood on the ground," he says, as if the answer is obvious.

"Did Lux check out?" I ask.

Mr. Ishmael looks left, then right, then left again. He's taking too long, so Vanessa shocks him and he falls to his knees.

"What is going on around here?" Mr. Sanders helps him up.

"That girl took off in the morning before we woke up," says Mr. Ishmael breathlessly.

"Did you *see* her take off?"

Mr. Ishmael removes a handkerchief from his back pocket and dabs his forehead. I'm not picking up any murderous vibes from him, but I am catching a hint of embarrassment and small amount of guilt. "I didn't see her check out, no."

"Did Mrs. Ishmael see?"

"No, she didn't. When I saw the blood, I had to clean it up before she came in."

Vanessa throws her hands up in the air. "For the love of

everything that is true crime, does this man not think to call the police when there's blood on the ground!"

Yes, he did. I'm seeing the scenario in his thoughts. He woke up early in the morning and shuffled to the kitchen to start the coffee machine. He looked out the window as he was filling up the pot and noticed Lux's car was no longer in the driveway. Odd, given it was barely five in the morning and she'd told him her plans of spending the next day exploring the town. There was nothing in Fernn Valley worth exploring before the sun came up. He checked her room. First knocking on the door. The handle was locked, but he had a hunch she'd taken off. This had happened to them before. Two weeks earlier, a girl had stayed the night and skipped out on them without paying. I can see the girl's image. Mr. Ishmael remembers her well because she was a cute girl with wavy blonde hair, blue eyes, a pretty smile, and a butterfly tattoo on her ankle. He couldn't believe the nerve of kids these days stealing from him. Angry, he unlocked the door to Lux's room and found the window ajar and a few blood spots on the floor. He told himself that Lux had gone out the window and cut herself in an attempt to skip out on having to pay. But deep down, he knew something wasn't right. He had to clean the blood before Mrs. Ishmael woke. Seeing the blood would trigger an ... *episode.* A few days later he heard there was a woman in town looking for her daughter. He wondered if there could be a connection, but never said anything. Again, he told himself that it was just a young girl who stole from him. The blood was from when she climbed out of the window. Nothing sinister had happened. The was no use starting rumors.

Mr. Ishmael is not a killer, but he did make a very poor judgment call.

"Fine, you didn't kill anyone. Sorry for throwing that out there," I say. "Why did you have to clean up the blood before Mrs. Ishmael saw?"

“Because ... *you know*. Lolly."

"Who the fetch is Lolly?" I ask.

"You don't know?" Mr. Sanders asks.

"If she knew, then she wouldn't be asking!" Vanessa storms towards the exit, waving for me to follow. "Let's talk to the brains."

I follow Vanessa, and Mr. Sanders and Mr. Ishmael follow me, and we all go back to the dry cleaners. Mrs. Ishmael is in the same spot, dabbing at her eyes with a wadded-up tissue. When she sees Mr. Sanders, her face goes tomato red, and she charges towards the man with murder in her eyes.

So Vanessa shocks her.

"Stop that," I hiss.

Mrs. Ishmael is barely phased by Vanessa's touch. If anything, she appears more focused. "You have a lot of nerve showing your face around here," she says to Mr. Sanders. Ouch. Her tone could break glass.

"Honey," Mr. Ishmael tries to calm his wife.

"Don't *honey* me!" She shoves her husband out of the way. "This man killed Whiskers!"

I climb up on a chair and clap my hands. "Everyone, shut up!"

There's a hushed silence, and all attention is on me. Good. "A young girl named Lux Piefer checked into your home the day of the book festival, and she never checked out. I need every ounce of information you have on her!"

“Oh, my." Mrs. Ishmael brings her hand to her chest. "I have no idea what you're talking about."

"I do." Mr. Ishmael steps forward. "It was that young girl with the camera who wanted to stay and explore Fernn Valley."

"That rings a bell," Mrs. Ishmael says. "Was she from Portland?"

"Yes," says Mr. Ishmael. "I never told you this, because I

didn't want to upset you. But she didn't actually check out. I found the room empty the next morning."

"And you found blood under the window," I remind him.

"Blood under the window?" Mrs. Ishmael bursts into tears. "In Lolly's room!" She smacks her husband upside the head. "Why didn't you tell me?"

Mr. Ishmael cowers. "I was scared you'd have one of your episodes."

She smacks him again. "Crying is not an *episode*. It's part of the grieving process!"

"Okay, who is Lolly?" I ask.

"Pollyanna was my niece. We called her Lolly. She was staying with us for a few months before she ... well, she took her life."

I'm frantically grabbing pieces of everyone's thoughts and putting them together to make a complete picture. Lolly was twenty-seven years old. She was divorced. No kids. She had a jovial personality and a bright smile. Mrs. Ishmael found her hanging in the closet. She left her laptop on the counter with a letter saying good-bye. This happened around the holidays. About six months before Lux disappeared.

Mrs. Ishmael smacks her husband on the backside of the head again, still crying. "I can't believe you didn't tell me! Did you call the police?"

"No," he says and winces, ready for the next bang to the head. "In our defense, it wasn't a lot of blood. It was little splatters. And we'd had one other girl check in and skip on us the month before."

"We really should collect money upfront," says Mrs. Ishmael as an afterthought.

"I need the name of the other girl!" I jump down off the chair. "She had blonde hair and a butterfly tattoo."

"How do you know that?" Mr. Ishmael asks.

"I just do! What is her name?"

"There's no need to shout, Zoe," says Mrs. Ishmael, dabbing at her eyes with a tissue. "Come by the house later, and I'll get it for you."

"No. I need it now. Right now! Give it to me."

"Do you want me to shock her?" Vanessa asks.

I give a small shake of my head.

"Are you unwell?" Mr. Sanders asks.

"No. I need the name. Right now!"

"I don't know that I can get that for you." Mrs. Ishmael looks at her husband. "Is it against HIPAA?"

"HIPAA is for doctors." I'm so freaking frustrated I feel punching a wall. *Gah!* "Just give me a first name."

Mrs. Ishmael thinks. "It was Britney ... no ... it was Brinkley. You know what? I'm not sure. She was from Texas."

Not super helpful, but a start. "What was her last name?"

"It's Sutton. Why? What are you planning to do?" Mrs. Ishmael gasps. "You're not writing an article on this are you? Cause I don't want my house wrapped in scandal."

Too late.

One twenty-something who committed suicide. One twenty-something who disappeared. One twenty-something who was killed. All happened within a six-month period.

Math was never my best subject, but I see a scary pattern here.

"Bye!" I push open the door and start to leave then remember. "Has anyone seen Brian Windsor within the last thirty minutes?"

They all shake their heads and look at each other. "I've been here all day," says Mr. Ishmael. "I did hear about his girlfriend."

"What happened?" asked Mrs. Ishmael.

"She's the one who ran over the welcome sign and died."

"Oh, sweet mother of goodness." Mrs. Ishmael crosses herself. "The entire town is cursed."

It's starting to feel that way. I ask them to text or call me if they happen to see Brian and then I leave, pushing the door open with more force than is required. The sidewalks are crowded. Everyone is out and about, enjoying this hot day.

"We're going to talk to Dominick now?" Vanessa asks, struggling to keep up.

"No." I open my car and get in. "I'm going to contact Lolly Sutton first."

Vanessa appears in the passenger seat. "Shouldn't we keep to the plan and move on to step two? The plan is set in place to prevent us for chasing white rabbits."

By white rabbits, she means leads that go nowhere. I've read all the Hot Cop series, so I'm well acquainted with the term. "Sorry, I need to talk to Lolly first. What if her death wasn't an actual suicide? With her death and Britney slash Brinkley and Lux disappearing all within six months, it's too much of a coincidence not to look into."

"I want to be sure we're keeping our focus on priority one. Keeping Brian alive."

"Of course we are. The best way to keep Brian alive was to catch the killer before he kills again. I need to contact Lolly to make sure." I drive across the street to Earl Park and park. "Stay here. I need a minute alone."

"Why? I want to hear."

"It's easier for me to connect to spirits when I'm not being watched." I stumble out of the car and take the pathway to the pond. Earl Park was named after our town's founder, Earl Fernn. I love the park. It reminds me of the setting from a sweet romance story: large willow trees, beveled walkways, a beautifully constructed gazebo, and a pond with a family of ducks that fly in every spring.

There isn't anyone here, which is unusual given the weather. But I'm grateful.

I take a seat on the bench inside the gazebo, close my eyes, and envision a door. The door is surrounded by bright rays of light. I first ask for Lux and wait. She's still not responding, but I can sense she's there. I don't know why she doesn't want to speak to me. So I ask for Lolly Sutton and wait ... and wait ... and wait ... and wait ...

I'm about to give up when there's a chill down my spine, and I'm overcome with the most joyful spirit I've ever felt before. I can't see Lolly, but her words fill my head.

Howdy-ho there. What can I do for you?

"Thank you for talking to me," I say.

I've always wanted to be summoned. It's quite exciting.

"Did you kill yourself or were you killed?" I feel intrusive coming right out and asking, but time is of the essence here.

Oh, sweetie, no I didn't. There was far too much to live for. I feel simply awful about my poor aunt thinking I killed myself. Can you tell her for me?

Aha! I knew she wasn't a white rabbit. "Yes, I will. Who killed you and made it look like a suicide?"

Oh, sweetie, I don't know. It doesn't really matter does it? I'm dead. There's nothing we can do to change that.

"How did you transition without finding out who killed you?"

It didn't matter to me.

"Well, it matters to me." I realize that I sound a bit judgy, but how can she not care? "What is the last thing you remember?"

I was lying in bed reading when there was a tap on my window. I pulled back the curtains to see what it is, and there wasn't anyone there. Then, poof, I was here.

"Do you have *any* idea who killed you?"

I couldn't tell you.

"What about neighbors, or your ex-husband, or people around town that you didn't get along with?"

Like I said, I couldn't tell you. Our neighbors were nice, and I had a good relationship with my ex-husband. I didn't have any beef with anyone in town. It's a mystery.

"There might be another girl there who was killed by the same person," I say. "Her name is either Brinkley or Britney. She was from Texas and has blonde hair and blue eyes. I don't know how it works there exactly, but do you think you can ask around?"

You just described about every third person here.

"Is that a no?"

It's unlikely.

Shoot. "If you happen to see a girl named Lux Piefer, please have her contact me, too."

I will. Good luck.

"Thank you," I say, and she's gone.

Looks like we just added at least one more murder to our list.

CHAPTER EIGHT

I'm not panicking. Even though it appears we are now hunting down a serial killer. I am not going to panic. I'm going to put my panic in a jar, and I'm going to seal that jar, and I'm going to stick that jar in a safe, and I'm going to lock that safe, and I'm going to drop that safe into the Pacific Ocean, and then I'm going to write a book and call it the *Panic in a Jar Method* and never panic again.

No panicking.

When I get back to my car, I find Vanessa meditating.

"I talked to Lolly," I say as I slide into my seat. "It wasn't suicide. She doesn't remember the details, and she doesn't want to know them ... I ... tried Lux ... again ... and she didn't answer!" Okay. I'm still not panicking.

What I am is beyond panicked. I'm in an altered freak-out state where the world is spinning and I can't feel my feet.

"Breathe, Zoe." Vanessa is showing me how it's supposed to work by inhaling and exhaling slowly. "Release the toxins and pull in purity."

"I don't understand what you're saying!" I grip the steering wheel and concentrate on the BMW symbol. "I think we need to explore the possibility that whoever killed Lolly also killed Britney/Brinkley and Lux and is the person you were talking to when you died. That's a lot of people!"

"Are you telling me that we're hunting down a serial killer?" Vanessa sounds way too excited about this.

So much so that I have to ask, "Do you even know what a serial killer is?"

"I'm going to pretend you didn't ask me that. Can you imagine what the headline will read if my last act here on earth was catching a serial killer? Wait. Wait." Vanessa pretends to splash water on her face. "I've lost focus. Brian. He is our main priority. On to step two. Dominick."

"Right. First I want to drive by the Ishmaels' house and get a lay of the land."

"Why do you keep inserting steps into our nine-step plan? We're taking too long!"

"Because I want to find Brian!"

"Why are you yelling at me!"

"Because I'm stressed out!"

"Then put your stress in a receptacle!"

"You can shove your receptacle where the sun doesn't shine!"

Vanessa inhales. "You take that back!"

"No!"

She shocks me, and I settle down. Feels more like a little jolt of energy, certainly not the crippling production Mr. Sanders and Mr. Ishmael made it out to be. Oddly enough, the shock forces my brain to refocus. I'm good. Now, Brian. "We *are* going to drive by the Ishmaels' house on our way to see Dominick." Except, I don't know where the Ishmaels live.

Time to call Mike.

I put him on speaker. "Please tell me the future has changed?" I ask as soon as he answers.

"Not yet. It's the same, and it's not as foggy anymore."

"What does that mean?" Vanessa asks.

Mike doesn't respond. "Vanessa wants to know what that means."

"I think it's becoming more set in stone."

"Fan-freaking-tastic!" Vanessa drops her head into her hands.

"The good news is that I just ran into a bunch of buddies from the softball team," says Mike. "They've got illegal fireworks from Oregon, and they're lighting them up tonight. I think that explains the bombs and gunfire we hear."

Oh, thank goodness. What a relief. I wondered what we could have possibly done to create a riot or war in Fernn Valley. "What time is this happening?"

"They're meeting at the softball field at eight."

I slump in the seat. "Eight o'clock gives us exactly four hours. Did you find Brian?"

"No. I've got everyone looking for him. Last I heard he was seen at the tow yard, demanding to speak to my uncles. They weren't there. My Aunt Berthy said Brian sped away. No one has seen him since."

"Where could he have gone?" I ask Vanessa.

"Sometimes he drives to clear his head."

Crap. My insides shrivel, and I feel sick. If Brian is driving around aimlessly, clearing his head, then it's going to be a lot more difficult to locate him.

"Where are you now?" I ask Mike.

"I'm at Butter Bakery. I just talked to Mrs. Muffin. She was on her way to Trucker this morning, and Vanessa swerved out in front of her. She said Vanessa had the phone in her hand and was texting and yelling and eating a fudge pop. There was no one else in the car. Mrs. Muffin called nine-one-one and was on the phone with the police when Vanessa crashed into the welcome sign and smashed into the tree."

"I don't eat ice cream!" Vanessa bellows into my eardrum, and I wince. "I don't eat dairy!"

"Maybe that's one of the reasons you were driving so erratically?" I offer. "You were having stomach troubles."

Vanessa shocks me.

"I feel bad for poor Mrs. Muffin. She's traumatized," Mike says. "When she went to check on Vanessa, she was already dead. She must have hit her head just right."

"I'm traumatized, too," says Vanessa. "I'm such an idiot. I can't believe I basically killed myself while eating ice cream."

"You're not an idiot."

"I didn't say I was," says Mike.

"I wasn't talking to you. I was talking to Vanessa. You can't hear her through the phone?"

"No. I couldn't hear her when we were alone at Brian's house either. I think I need to be with you. I've decided that you're a spirit conduit."

"I have a different theory," Vanessa says. "I'll tell you after we save Brian."

Okay. Anyway. "At least we know Vanessa was alone in the car and where the fudge pop wrapper came from. Now we need to find out who she was talking to."

"It sounds like I was talking to a serial killer!"

Oh, that's right. I tell Mike what we discovered about Lolly, and Lux, and another girl from Texas.

"Dude, that's intense," he says.

That's one word for it. "I'm at Earl Park. Do you know where the Ishmaels' house is?"

“It's ... nawt ... faaarrr." His voice is muffled. "I'll text you the address."

"Are you eating?" I ask.

"Uh ... yes," he says sheepishly. "I was hungry. Sorry?"

"No need to apologize. I get it." I'd probably be hungry too if I wasn't actively trying not to have a meltdown. "Please call me if you find Brian or if the future changes. Okay?"

"Ten-four, boss."

As soon as I hang up, my phone pings with an incoming text. It's the Ishmaels' address. Mike wasn't kidding. They live one block from Earl Park on a quiet tree-lined street with Victorian-style houses. The Ishmaels' home is blue with white trim and stands three stories high. There are two rocking chairs sitting on the wraparound porch and a white picket fence so bright it looks freshly painted.

I keep the car running and stumble outside. Vanessa floats through the door, and we stand side by side on the sidewalk, staring up at the massive home.

"The fact that we could have multiple murders happening in this one place rules out anyone passing through town," says Vanessa. "Whoever is killing these girls knows the layout of the house, where guests sleep, when guests are here, and how to get in. You said there was blood by the window, right?"

"Yes, and Lolly said she heard a tap on the window."

"Then the window must be the point of entrance," Vanessa says. "And you're sure it wasn't Mr. Ishmael?"

"If it is, he's really good at hiding his thoughts. Though I seriously doubt it. He's not that strong-minded or just *strong*. He dropped like a fly when you touched him."

"I have that effect on men. Always have."

I laugh at what I think is a joke, but a quick look at her face tells me she's being serious.

"Brian and I first met at a sorority party," she says, her voice distant. "The house looked similar to this one, except not as well-kept. I was playing beer pong with friends, and this guy comes up and starts talking to me. He kept pushing his glasses up his nose, and I could tell he was totally nervous." She laughs at the memory. "He talked about giraffes. How they can run thirty-five miles per hour, how their legs are longer than most humans are tall, how their necks are too short to reach the ground ... he was such a dork and yet so damn endearing. I couldn't help myself."

I catch a few glimpses of her memory. Happy memories that are now shadowed by sorrow.

"Anyway." Vanessa rolls her shoulders. "You better treat that man well, or I'll come back and haunt your scrawny—"

"What are you doing here!" Tanner is standing on the patio, wearing a plain white T-shirt and a hat made of foil.

"I'm trying to figure out who killed Lux," I say. "What's with the aluminum?"

"So you can't read my thoughts," he says.

Vanessa rolls her eyes. "I can't *even* with this guy."

Neither can I.

"Ask what room she was in," Vanessa says.

"Can we see the room she stayed in?"

"Who is *we*?" he asks.

Oh. That's right. "I meant *me*."

Tanner is reluctant at first but eventually agrees to show us around after Vanessa shocks him.

The entryway is grand with a straight staircase and an old-house smell. The chandelier hanging over a circular wooden table has amber glass with teardrop crystals dangling from the bottom. Everything is wood from the baseboards, to the crown molding, to the staircase, to the floors, to the ceiling. Lots and lots of mahogany wood.

Tanner takes us through a sitting area, down a hall, past an office, and into a room with a four-post bed and a cream-colored vanity with little roses painted around the mirror. I recognize the room from Mr. Ishmael's and Tanner's thoughts.

"This is it," Tanner says and pulls open the curtains. It's

really hard to take him seriously with that aluminum foil hat on. "Do you see any ghosts?"

Just one.

The room is lovely at first glance. Once I step in, the little hairs on the back of my neck stand up. The lone rocking chair in the corner with a porcelain doll, the cobwebs gathering in the corners, even the way the dust particles dance in the rays of light peeking in through the window is eerie. I have a feeling of distress and uneasiness the further I step in.

Vanessa is examining the window. "This has a crank. It would be difficult for someone to pry it open from the outside." She walks through the wall and is now outside.

"And Lolly was found in the closet?" I ask Tanner.

"Mmhmm." He points to a door and takes a step back, knocking into the vanity.

I'm not going to lie, there's a niggle in the pit of my stomach, and I half expect to open the door and find a disturbed spirit rocking in the fetal position while clutching a doll chanting "this house is ours" or something equally as creepy.

Much to my relief, inside there is nothing but a few lone hangers. The closet is the size of a small room, and the spirit of distress is so strong it's almost tangible. I can almost feel the evil crawling up my arms like little cockroaches.

Blahahaha.

"Question." Vanessa suddenly appears, and I scream.

"What did you find?" Tanner asks from the other side of the room. He's practically willed himself to become one with the cream-colored wallpaper.

"Nothing." I grip my chest.

"Ask who the next-door neighbors are," Vanessa says.

"Who are your next-door neighbors?" I ask Tanner.

"Uh ... to the right are the Krasinskis."

Here's what I know about the Mr. and Mrs. Krasinski: They're like a hundred years old.

"To the left are the Dashers," says Tanner.

Here's what I know about the Dashers: They're even older than the Krasinskis.

"What about across the street?" Vanessa asks.

"Tanner, can you give me a rundown of everyone who lives in the neighborhood," I ask to save time.

"Can't you do a full town sweep with your powers and read everyone's mind?" he asks. "Wouldn't that be easier?"

"It doesn't work like that."

"We could build you a suit that enhances your superpowers," he suggests, and he's being serious.

"No. I'm not an Avenger. I'm a medium. Who lives in the neighborhood?"

Tanner shrugs. "It's mostly a lot of retired people." He runs down the list and, yeah, it's like all of Fernn Valley's most seasoned residents live on this street. Not that old people can't be serial killers. It's just that it's probably harder to pull it off when you use a walker.

I write down each name anyway in my phone. You never know.

"Can you think of anyone else who died here?" I ask.

"Lolly is the only one I know of. We've only lived here a year, though," says Tanner.

"Zoe!" Vanessa is in the closet. "Come here."

Ugh. I'd rather not go in there again, but I do it anyway. Vanessa is in the corner, and she points to the floor, which are planks of mahogany wood.

"Stomp your foot," she says.

I do as told.

"Now stomp over there." She points to different plank. "Keep stomping around."

"Does that dance get rid of demons?" asks Tanner, cowering in the doorway.

"Sure," I say, still clomping around. It's easier than explaining the truth. Not that I know the truth. Vanessa is lying down with her ear pressed to the floor.

"Stop!"

I pause with my right foot up.

"Lift this floorboard," she says.

"I drop to my hands and knees and try to get a grip on the wood, but it's not budging. "Can you get me a butter knife?" I ask Tanner. "I need to lift this floorboard."

"Uh ... hold on." He leaves and returns with a crowbar. "Will this work?"

"Sure." I snatch the crowbar from his grasp. The floorboard is nailed down good, and it takes all the strength I have to break it free. Underneath we find cement. "Wow, that's interesting." And a total waste of time.

"Try that one." Vanessa points to another floorboard.

"Uh ... Zoe? Is tearing up my parents' flooring part of the getting rid of demons process?"

"Sure." I pry up the next floorboard, and the next, and the next. More cement. More cement. More cement. I feel like screaming this is such a waste of time, but I can feel that Vanessa believes she's onto something.

I shove the crowbar under another floorboard and use all my might to lift, only to fall back on my butt. The crowbar flies out of my hand and almost takes out Tanner. Who has been watching wide-eyed and totally freaked out in the doorway the entire time.

"Aha!" Vanessa yells triumphantly. "There it is."

I remove the floorboard with ease and find a hole. Two more floorboards removed, and I'm staring down a secret exit. "Go down there," Vanessa says.

"Uh, why don't you go and give me a full report."

"I don't want to go down a hole," Tanner says.

"I wasn't talking to you."

"Oh. Gotcha. Are you talking to the demons?" Tanner asks.

"Sure."

Vanessa shocks me.

"I mean, *no*," I say.

"Seriously! If you want something done right!" Vanessa stares at the hole and purses her lips. "I could have gone through the floor instead of tearing up all the wood. That would have been the smarter move."

"Yes, it would have," I agree.

Vanessa taps her forehead as if to say *duh*. "I'm still not used to being able to walk through walls." She floats down into the tunnel and crawls out of site.

"Do you think that's like one of those secret tunnels they used to help slaves escape?" Tanner asks.

"Probably not."

Vanessa returns. "It leads to a secret door right under the window! I can't open it, obviously, but it blends in with the house. You wouldn't know it was there unless you knew it was there. Our killer probably tapped on that window to create a distraction then snuck in through this secret tunnel to execute his attack."

I do a full body shiver and turn around. "Tanner, who owned this house before your parents bought it?"

"Uh ... I don't know. Your parents would. They were the realtors."

"Yes, and so would yours since they bought it." I don't want to involve my parents in any way shape or form. Who knows? They might end up in the forest too.

Tanner takes out his phone and sends a quick text to his mom. "She says it was bank owned."

"Oh, come on!" Vanessa throws her hands up in the air. "This is Fernn Valley, everyone knows everyone. Someone has to know who used to live here!"

"Uh ... my mom says this was a bed and breakfast before the bank took possession of it," he says, reading the text. "The family that owned it lived out of town."

"This is not helpful!" Vanessa hollers into Tanner's ear, and he jumps.

"I need to find out who used to own this place, who ran the bed and breakfast, anything. I need the information on anyone who stayed here. Can you find that for me?" I ask Tanner.

"Y-yeah, sure. Will that get rid of the demons?"

Vanessa shocks him, and he falls to his knees.

"Yes," I say and step around him. "Please call me ASAP with the information."

"Wait," Vanessa says. "Take a picture of the floor first. For the cops and for the article."

I step around Tanner, snap a picture, and we're off.

Vanessa and I are back in my car, driving to the Food Mart. The evil presence in the Ishmaels' guest room was so real I feel like I need a shower. To think about what horrible things could have happened there makes me physically ill.

"I want my phone first," says Vanessa. "We're running out of time. Even if Dominick has information, there's going to be a lot of talking, and I'm tired of talking. Screw the steps. I want to take action. If we have my phone then we can see who I was talking to when I drove off the road."

"I'm not sure how to legally obtain the phone." Or illegally for that matter. "Let's get an update from Mike. He could have the money by now, and he might remember who owned the

Ishmaels' house before it was repossessed." Using the controls on my steering wheel, I call Mike. His voicemail answers on the first ring. Dang it.

"Why didn't he answer?" Vanessa demands.

"I don't know. He could be on the other line. I think we should go talk to Dominick right now."

"We need my phone. This is a matter of life or death. Oh!" She gasps so loudly *I* almost drive off the road. "I have an idea. You're going to hate it, but you're going to do it anyway."

I'm scared to ask.

"You're going to call my dad. He can call the coroner's office and release my personal effects to you."

"Why would he do that if he's never met me?"

"Because we'll blackmail him."

She can't be serious. "I'm not blackmailing anyone!"

"It's either blackmail or money. You don't have money, we have two and a half hours, so blackmail it is. I told you that you wouldn't like my idea, but it's the only way. You're going to call him and say you know about his offshore accounts and you're willing to keep your mouth quiet if he hands over my personal effects. That's it."

"That's it? You've got to be kidding me. The last person to confront your father about the offshore accounts is dead."

"This is true. I hadn't thought of that ..." She bites her nails. "Aha! Mike will know if you're going to die, so you can escape."

"Gee, thanks."

"Do you have a better plan? Because that sun looks awfully low in the sky, and if Brian Windsor dies, I will *never* forgive you."

"This is *such* a bad idea."

"It's a *terrible* idea, but the only one I've got."

My gut tells me this is stupid. But my mouth says, "Fine."

I'll do anything to save Brian.

We drive to the coroner's office, and I park under a tree. "I think I'm going to have a nervous breakdown," I say, my phone in my hand on speaker. The line rings, and I bite my lip to the point I can taste blood in my mouth.

"Don't doubt yourself, Zoe."

"Okay. I have *no doubt* that I'm going to have a nervous breakdown." The line continues to ring, and I say a silent prayer that her father doesn't answer.

But of course he does.

"This is Max," he says. Max Tobin has a hard-hearted voice.

Vanessa urges me to speak. We'd done a quick rehearsal of what I had to say on our drive over. Except, the words have eluded me. "Hello, Mr. Tobin. I am so sorry to hear about your daughter."

Vanessa makes a strangled sound and wrings her hands. "Stick to the script," she hisses.

Right.

"Who is this?" Max demands. "Why are you calling me from a blocked number?"

Oh, good. It worked. Vanessa said that if I hit star-six-seven before I dialed, it would block my number.

"My name is not important right now. What is important is that I know about your offshore accounts and the murder of your daughter's grandmother."

There's silence on the other end.

"Hello?"

"You have my attention," he says.

"Keep going," Vanessa says.

"You and I can help each other out. I need Vanessa's personal effects from the coroner's office in exchange for my silence." *Gah,* I can't believe those words just came out of my mouth.

"I call your bluff," says Max. "And if you think for one

second that I will let you near my kid's stuff, then you're out of your mind. I will find you. I will catch you. I will kill you."

Uhhhh ... this reaction was not part of the script.

Vanessa shakes her head. "Tell him that you call *his* bluff."

I really don't want to.

But I do it anyway.

"Oh yeah, well ... I call your bluff."

"If you think I am bluffing, then you have no idea who you are messing with. Go ahead and spill whatever information you want. You will touch my daughter's belongings over my dead body."

My eyes slide to Vanessa. She's both frustrated and furious.

I'm feeling both miserable and guilty. I shouldn't have let Vanessa talk me into blackmail.

"Mr. Tobin," I say with a sigh. "I'm not the blackmailing type. What I am is a personal friend of Vanessa's. She and I were working on a story together, and I think she was really close to solving it. What I need is the information that's on her phone and her laptop. If you could, please call the coroner's office right now and do whatever it is that you need to do so I can get that. I promise to return all her things tomorrow ... hello?" I check my phone to be sure we're still connected.

"What is your name?" he asks.

"My name is Zoe Lane. I live here in Fernn Valley, where Vanessa was killed."

Vanessa slaps her forehead. "You had one job! And that was not to give your name and location right away!"

I ignore her. "Also ... I-I-I can see Vanessa. I'm a medium. I know that sounds ridiculous, but it's the truth. Vanessa's spirit is here. She's disgusted by your illegal dealings. How could you hurt her grandma? She doesn't want to believe it. She wants to remember you as her daddy. She wants to remember that time when she was ten and you took her on a special daddy-daughter trip to San Francisco. How she got carsick and you stopped at this little mini-mart so you could clean up the mess. And the woman who ran it had a beard, and Vanessa wouldn't stop gawking ..."

Vanessa is staring at me. "Oh, hell. Abort mission. Hang up the phone. Stop talking right now. That is not what I said at all."

No, it's not. It's what she was thinking. I need to stay true to myself, and my true self does not want to blackmail anyone ... anymore.

I'm pretty sure Max has hung up on me, until I hear him breathing. "You said your name was Zoe Lane?"

I *really* wish I could see his thoughts and feel his feelings over the phone. "Yes," I say.

"Faux fur," Vanessa blurts out. "Tell him faux fur!"

"Uh ... faux fur." I have no idea what this means, and it takes Max Tobin quite a few minutes to process this.

"Did you kill Vanessa?" he asks.

Oh, geez. "No! Not at all. I have countless alibis—" I stop myself before I say prison was one of them. "Vanessa's death was an accident. She is with me, and she said, 'faux fur,' even though I don't know what that means." I look at her.

"He told me when I was in high school that if I was ever in a situation where I needed help. To call and say, 'faux fur,' and he'd pick me up. That was our safe phrase. Hopefully that will get him to listen."

Oh. Clever. "We need the laptop and phone, please."

"I'm making arrangements for her to be transported back to Portland." His voice is low, and I don't know if he's talking to himself or me. "This doesn't make any sense ... what color was her favorite hairbrush in second grade."

I look at Vanessa.

"The brush wasn't a color. It had The Little Mermaid on the back."

"It was a Little Mermaid brush," I say, hopeful this will provide the proof he needs.

"Okay," he finally says. "I will call the coroner's office right now, and I will ask them to release her cell phone and laptop to you. I want it back tomorrow, and you will erase nothing. Do you understand me?"

"Absolutely." I smile triumphantly and give Vanessa a *told ya we didn't need to blackmail* look.

"Yeah, well, make sure Mike keeps an eye on your future. That's all I'm going to say."

Gulp.

We hang up and wait a few minutes before we go inside the building, allowing Max enough time to make the arrangements. My right leg bounces as I watch the clock.

"Do you actually love him?" Vanessa asks out of the blue.

"Are we talking about Brian?"

"No, Tanner! Honestly. Yes. Brian. Do you love him?"

"We don't know each other that well. I *really* like him."

"How did this whole thing between you two start?"

Oh, geez. "Do you really want to talk about this right now?"

"I wouldn't ask you if I didn't."

Okay. Fair enough. "The truth is nothing has started. I'd seen his picture printed in *The Gazette*, and I thought he was dreamy almost in a Clark Kent kind of way. Back then I didn't get out of the house much. My parents kept me sheltered because they thought I was a schizophrenic. The first time I ever did anything for myself was when I interviewed for an entry-level position at *The Gazette* over six months ago. Brian didn't offer me the job, and I ended up seeing my first spirit that day. Well, my first spirit that I could remember. I'd conversed with the dead when I was a toddler. Anyway. Eventually I was offered a job, and we have worked together. Nothing ever happened between us until today."

Vanessa crosses her legs and stares straight ahead. "What about Mike?"

"What about him?"

"I have a theory."

"So you said. I thought you weren't going to tell me until we save Brian."

"I've changed my mind." She shifts in her seat to face me. "I think you two are connected, and that's why he can hear me only when he's around you. And you can see his visions."

I hadn't thought about it that way.

"Here's the thing, Zoe Lane. Brian is a great guy, and you'd be lucky to have him. Brian is sensitive and takes things to heart. Even though we broke up, my death is going to be hard on him. Don't enter into a relationship unless you're sure that you won't break his heart by running off with someone else."

I'm about to ask whom I would ever run off with when I realize she's talking about Mike.

"Vanessa, I won't break his heart. Mike and I are medium partners. That's it."

"So long as you're sure," she says and checks the time. "Let's go get my phone."

CHAPTER NINE

My stomach is a mess of nerves as we walk into the coroner's office. Zeke is leaning back in his chair with his feet propped up on the desk. This time, he's playing a game on his phone.

"I'm here to collect Vanessa Tobin's things," I say. "Her father should have called."

"Her father?" Zeke sits up and rolls his chair to his desk and checks the computer. "I don't see anything in the system." He lifts the office phone to his ear and dials an extension.

I fidget with my thumbs while I wait, praying that we've done enough to change the future.

Zeke hangs up the phone. "Mr. Tobin just called, and he requested that we hand over Vanessa's personal property to you. However, he does need to give us permission in writing. He promised to send over a notarized letter. Apparently this is an urgent situation?"

"Yes. Very urgent. Can't you just take his word for it?"

Zeke shakes his head. "Come back in thirty minutes."

Ugh! "Fine." I start to storm away then think better of it. "Thank you for your help," I say nicely. Then I storm away, feeling frustrated and flustered and faint and a whole bunch of other adjectives that start with an F.

My phone rings as soon as we get back to my car. It's Mike. I put the call on speaker and answer, "Hello."

"Future is still the same," Mike says.

That has got to be the worst greeting of all time. "I'm glad you called. Do you know who owned the Ishmaels' house before the bank repossessed it?" I ask then retell the tale of the creepy old house, Tanner's aluminum hat, and the secret tunnel.

"Dude, that's crazy, man. I know that house sat vacant for many years. I'm almost positive it was owned by a family who lived out of town and used it as a bed and breakfast. I'll ask around. In the meantime, I have good news and bad news. The bad news is that I still haven't found Brian and I can't withdrawal the money from the account my aunt set up for me. There is some confusion about who the primary account holder is. They said I'm going to have to wait until the manager is back on Monday. The good news is that I talked to Zeke about the amount. Dude, he meant ten bucks."

I blink. "Are you telling me that we could have obtained Vanessa's belongings for ten dollars?"

"Nah, he said the coroner would have let us *look* for ten bucks."

I feel like punching something. So I do. My steering wheel. For a big muscle car, the horn is pretty weak.

"No. No. No." Vanessa shakes her head so fast her face blurs. "Mike said ten *thousand*, and Zeke didn't correct him."

This is true. "Why didn't Zeke say '*hey man, dude, like we're talking dollars, dude. Not thousands?*'"

"He said that if we were willing to pay ten grand, he wasn't going to stop us. They don't get paid well."

I can't believe this. "You're telling me we could have looked at the phone hours ago for ten dollars?"

"Yes."

"Ten freaking dollars."

"Yes."

I drop my head into my hands. Ten dollars is still nine dollars more than I have, but Mike has a wallet full of twenties! We could have even left the coroner a tip! Ah! "We tried to blackmail Vanessa's father into giving us permission to take her personal effects," I say.

"You did what? Zoe! That is a terrible idea."

"Yes," I agree. "It was. I ended up chickening out and telling him I was a medium. Anyway, he's letting us have everything."

"That's not going to backfire."

"Is that a personal opinion or a vision?"

"Opinion, based on the fact that we think this man killed the last person to confront him." I can almost hear Mike rolling his eyes. "Anyway. While you were making *horrible* decisions, I was talking to Mrs. Vander."

Oh, good.

Here's what I know about Mrs. Vander: She is the same age as my mom, has a mole on her left cheek, and she always has a chunk of gum in her mouth. She also works at the sheriff station.

"Mrs. Vander remembers the day Jolene came into the office to report her daughter's disappearance," Mike says. "Vance was convinced Lux had taken off. He even had Mrs. Vander look up all the gas stations and rest stops between here and San Francisco. According to her, he didn't appear stressed or like he was covering anything. She really doesn't think he had anything to do with Lux's disappearance."

Honestly, I don't either. He was worth looking into, though.

"It's not him," Vanessa says. "It doesn't sound right."

"Do you remember anything?" I ask.

"No. It's still a blank, but my gut is telling me it's not Sheriff Vance." She bites her nails. "Let's go talk to Dominick. He very well could have been one of the last people to see me alive. I don't remember even buying the ice cream."

Good idea. I say good-bye to Mike with the promise that I won't attempt to blackmail anyone else.

It takes five minutes to get to the Food Mart. The ice cream truck is parked on the side of the building.

Perfect.

Inside, it smells of day-old hot dogs, stale coffee, and BO, since just about everyone is there stocking up on ice cream and popsicles. Working the register is a teenager girl with braces and red hair. Even though she's ringing up a customer, I grab her attention.

"Where is Dominick?" I ask.

"He's in the stock room, getting ready to take the truck out once more," she says with a smile.

"Thank you." I go outside and walk around to the back entrance. The door is open, and Dominick is inside pulling boxes of popsicles from a walk-in freezer.

I knock on the open door.

Dominick looks up and wipes his forehead with the back of his hand. "Can I help you?" he asks.

"My name is Zoe Lane, and I have a few questions for you."

"Yeah, I know who you are. You've been here before, and you speak to dead people?"

“Uh ... I-I-I um."

"My dad said you zapped him earlier today."

"No. No. No zapping." I move out of the way to let Dominick walk past me with a dolly filled with boxes of chocolate-covered ice cream bars. He stops at the back of the truck, opens the door, and climbs in.

"He also said you were looking for a girl that disappeared from the Ishmaels' house," he says.

I hand him a box of ice cream cones. "I am. Her name was Lux Piefer. Do you know anything?"

"No, but seriously. I think the Ishmaels' house is haunted. Have you ever been in there?"

"Yes. It's *interesting*," I say, for lack of a better word.

"I visited Tanner when he first moved in with his parents and, damn, gave me the chills."

I hand him a box of popsicles. "Do you know who owned the place before them?"

"I can't remember their names. It was a family who lived out of town. They turned it into a bed and breakfast. It used to do real well. They'd get a lot of people who were just passing through town. The place went under when they opened the hotel on Main Street."

Shoot. I need to know the name of this family.

"Ask if he talked to me!" Vanessa bellows into my ear, taking me by surprise, and I drop a box of ice cream bars.

"You okay?" Dominick jumps down from the back of the truck and grabs ahold of my arm. "Dang, you're freezing."

"I-I-I'm fine. Fine. So sorry about the ice cream." I grab the box, which is now smashed and oozing. Oops.

"It's fine." He takes the ice cream bars from me and chucks them into the dumpster. "What happened to you?"

"I just got ... startled."

"By a ghost?"

Yep. "No. No. No."

"Also ask him about Gary Handhoff," Vanessa says again. "And since we're here, ask him if he killed me. There's no time to beat around the bush."

I don't need to ask Dominick if he killed anyone. He has a bright, breezy spirit. He is not a killer. "Have you had many interactions with Gary Handhoff?" Dominick runs the only Food Mart in town. He has to know everyone.

Dominick rolls his eyes. "Who hasn't had interactions with at least one of the Handhoff brothers? They don't come in here too much. Gary, he's the one with the rifle collection, right?"

"Yes," I say, remembering what Mike said about Gary liking to play with guns.

"I've purchased a few cars from Gary. I promised myself after the last time I would no longer give the Handhoffs my business."

"Because of the Self-Storage Place?"

"That and they give off creepy vibes. Except for Mike. He's a good guy." Dominick climbs back into the truck, and I hand him a box of waffle cones. "Do you think Gary Handhoff killed someone?"

Probably.

I hand Dominick a package of single serving vanilla ice cream cups, the kind with wooden sticks. I'm not sure why I'm standing here, loading ice cream. Could be Dominick's pleasant spirit is overpowering the evil feelings still lingering from the Ishmaels' guest room. Or it could be because Dominick is now thinking about Gary Handhoff. An image of a gold Civic hatchback with no plates comes into his mind. He'd offered Gary five hundred dollars, but he wouldn't take it. Said it wasn't for sale. Dominick is still irked by the incident. He really wanted that car.

"You saw a gold hatchback Honda Civic!" I blurt out, unable to help myself. "When did you see the car?"

"Seriously?" Dominick looks over his shoulders, as if expecting someone to be standing behind him. "How the heck did you know that? I-I-I ..." He starts to stutter, so Vanessa shocks him, and he falls to his knees. "Did you zap me?"

"No, but this is important. When did you see the car?"

Vanessa stands over him with her hand up and ready to shock.

"It was about ... s-six months ago?" he says. "But I was thinking that in my *head*. How did you get in my *head*?"

"I knew the Handhoffs were hiding something!" Vanessa stomps her foot. "Now ask him about the fudge pop."

"One more thing," I say to Dominick. "Do you sell fudge pops?"

"Uh ... yeah, yeah." Before I can stop him, he slides open the freezer and produces a fudge pop in a yellow wrapper. "T-take it. Take whatever you want."

Oh, geez. I take the ice cream from his shaky hand and look at Vanessa.

"That's the wrapper," she says.

"This morning, you were near Brian Windsor's house, and you sold a fudge pop to someone. Do you remember?"

He grimaces. "I heard about his girlfriend. That's terrible."

"It is," I say. "Did you sell a fudge pop to Vanessa?" I shake the ice cream at him.

"Yeah. She swerved over and parked right in front of my truck. She looked really tired, and she asked for anything made with soy because she's lactose intolerant. Then she was talking about a capsule? The fudge pop is all I have that's nondairy. I was ringing her up when she got a phone call. I told her the total, and she threw a five-dollar bill at me and rushed back to her car."

I stare down at the wrapper. Nondairy is displayed in small font under fudge pop. Oh, my gosh. My eyes dart toward Vanessa.

"I don't remember ... but then ... I kind of remember ..."

"Do you happen to know who she was talking to on the phone?" Long shot, yes, but it only happened this morning.

"Yeah, it was someone named Jolene. It caught my attention right away because my fiancée's name is Jolene, and when Vanessa answered the phone, she told Jolene to calm down, take a breath, and start over. Sounded urgent. Then Vanessa left in such a hurry I panicked. She wasn't talking to my Jolene, though. I called her after Vanessa left."

"Jolene!" I drop the fudge pop. "She was speaking to Jolene!"

"*Yes,*" Dominick says slowly. "You okay?"

"Holy hell." I turn around and race to my car. Vanessa is already in the passenger seat ready to go. "Do you remember talking to Jolene?"

"It sounds familiar. *Really* familiar. Crap, Zoe! What if Jolene was with the killer, and the killer was keeping her hostage, and when I died the killer ... I don't know. Somehow ... *Ugh.*" She massages her temples as if willing the memory to resurface. "It's like I can *almost* remember feeling rushed, like it was a matter of life or death ..."

"Let's get your phone and see if that brings some clarity."

CHAPTER TEN

I peel into the parking lot of the coroner's office. As soon as I run in, Zeke stands up.

"I have everything for you." He hands me a file box with a computer, cell phone, wallet, and purse. "Dude, so sorry about the ten dollars versus ten thousand thing. Bad call on my part. Handhoff is my man, and I don't mean to disrespect. We're cool, right?"

"Uh, sure. Why is there aluminum on your head?"

Zeke adjusts his foil hat. "I talked to Tanner."

"Of course you did."

I first roll my eyes then take Vanessa's belongings back to my car.

"First check my phone. What if I was on the phone with Gary Handhoff?" Vanessa gives me the passcode. "Now look at text messages."

I search through Vanessa's texts. "There aren't any messages sent or received this morning or around the time of the accident."

I check her call log. "There's an incoming call at ten forty-seven from Jolene. After you hung up, you immediately called a number in Trucker." I click on the call to get more information. "It looks like the call ended at eleven ten. Which is right about when you died."

Vanessa is mulling this over. "Mrs. Muffin said the phone was in my hand, and I was yelling. Which means that I was probably looking something up while I on the phone. Check and see if I looked up directions."

I click on the navigation app. "Last time you looked up an address was two weeks ago."

"Check my Internet history."

I click on the Internet icon. "Last thing you looked up was *Top Ten Signs Your Boyfriend is Cheating on You.*"

"Yeah, that's probably not it. Call Jolene first."

My thumb hoovers over Jolene's contact information. It's hard to imagine what will happen between now and sunset to make Jolene want to take a bullet for me. "If she and I never talk, then she won't know who I am. If she doesn't know who I am, then she can't go to the forest with me."

"Just call her!"

Yikes. Okay. "It's ringing," I say, Vanessa's phone at my ear. "I got voicemail. Should I leave a message?"

"No. Hang up and send her a text."

I hang up and compose a message saying I have information regarding Lux and ask her to call me right away. Then I add *don't come to Fernn Valley under any circumstances.*

"Good," Vanessa says. "New plan. Step one: call the Trucker number. I have no idea who that could be."

I call the number and press the phone to my ear. "It's the *Trucker Newspaper*. They're already closed for the day."

"Why on earth would I call the *Trucker Newspaper?*"

"Maybe Jolene found a clue in an article?"

"Then I'd email the reporter directly ..." She puffs her cheeks, deep in thought. "Who works for the paper that I know?"

"Elvin Peterson does. He was at the accident scene this morning taking pictures. Do you think you were yelling at him? He was on our list because I couldn't tell if he was giving off evil vibes."

"Give me a second." She squeezes her eyes closed and clasps her hands over her heart. "It's almost ... there."

My phone rings, and I set Vanessa's down. It's Mike. I make a silent plea that the future has changed.

"Everything is the same," he says as soon as I answer. "I still can't find Brian."

Dang it!

"Lori and Phil Stephens owned the house before it was repossessed. They lived in Trucker but had the house in Fernn Valley as a bed and breakfast. After the bank took possession, they moved to Delaware."

Shoot.

"The problem is we're running out of time, and my vision is clear now," he says.

"What does that mean?"

"I think it's happening no matter what. My other visions were foggy, but now I can see everything crystal clear."

"How?" I smack the steering wheel. "We have Vanessa's phone, and computer. We know there was a tunnel under the Ishmaels' guest room. We know it wasn't Dominick or Tanner or Mr. Ishmael. We don't think it was Sheriff Vance, and the former owners live on the other side of the country. I just found out that Lux's car was likely at the tow yard. Vanessa was right. Do you know where Gary is?"

"Calm down and back up," says Mike. "How do you know the car was in the tow yard?"

I tell him about my encounter with Dominick.

"I forgot Dom was engaged to a Jolene. I'm actually one of his groomsmen ... Anyway. He's had a lot of interaction with my uncles. He likes to buy old cars and fix them up. Do you think my uncle Gary is our guy?"

"Shhhh!" Vanessa hisses. "Lower your voice, I'm trying to concentrate."

Oops. "Can you see the killer now that your vision is crystal clear?" I whisper.

"The man has mud all over his face and hands, and I don't recognize him at all. He's beefier than anyone in my family." Mike's breathing quickens. "I'm going to the tow yard now. Hopefully my aunt will give me the deets."

"Are you running?"

"No, I'm at the park. I was looking for Brian ... crap!"

"Mike, what happened?" I ask in a panic. "Are you hurt?"

"No, the sprinklers just came on, and I'm soaked ..." his voice trails off. "I just took off my shirt."

"Why?"

"Because it's wet, and that was my first instinct. Hold on."

I hear him talking to someone. "Mike? Are you okay? Mike!"

"I'm back," he says. "I ... uh ... Hunter Krasinski is here."

"So?"

"He's passing out shirts for his band. They're playing tomorrow night."

"So?" I'm struggling to find the relevance.

"He just gave me the shirt from my vision. It has a clown on the front, and on the back it says *The Clown Attacks*."

Ah! "Don't put it on."

"Am I just supposed to walk around without a shirt?"

"No! Go home and get one," I say. Honestly.

"What if I'm supposed to wear this shirt?"

"Oh, hell!" Vanessa explodes. "It's a freaking shirt. If he wears the shirt, it's not going to kill him. Taking off the shirt is not going to kill him. What is going to save Brian's life is if you find him and tell him to stay out of the damn forest."

I relay this information to Mike.

"So I should put the shirt on?" he asks timidly.

Vanessa pretends to strangle someone.

"Wear whatever, Mike," I say. "Just please get to the tow yard and *be* careful."

"I'm on my way. But just to make sure, I should put the shirt on."

Oh, geez.

We all agree that the shirt is not going to change the outcome and hang up.

I check the time. *Ahhh!* We have less than an hour before sundown!

"Do you remember anything else?" I ask Vanessa.

"No! It's driving me nuts!" She thrusts her hands through her hair. "It's a complete injustice that the dead can't remember how they died. How do I file a formal complaint?"

"I don't know. Talk to God?"

She grunts. "We can do this. We *can* do this ... Zoe, write this down."

I grab my notebook and click my pen. "Ready!"

"We're going to make two columns. One of facts. One of feelings. Fact: I spoke to Jolene. She was upset. Then I called the Trucker paper. Feeling: the last person I talked to is the person who killed Lux. Fact: the person who shoots Brian is not anyone from around here, otherwise Mike would know him. He knows everyone. Fact-slash-educated-guess based on information obtained from Dominick: Lux's car was at the Handhoff tow yard."

"Should I start a new column for fact-slash-educated-guess?"

"Excellent question. Yes. Okay. Fact: Lolly and Lux were both killed in the Ishmaels' guest room. Fact-slash-educated-guess: the Texas girl was also killed. Fact: there is a tunnel under the house leading outside. Fact: Tanner was not involved. Fact: he's a total pansy."

"Tanner ... pansy ..." I repeat as I'm writing.

"Fact: you had a bad feeling about Gary Handhoff ... call Jolene again."

"Call Jolene ... again ..." I'm writing.

"No. Actually *call* her, now," she says.

"Right. Got it."

I call Jolene again, and again, and again, and again, and again. She's still not answering. I call Brian again, and again, and again, and again, and again. He's not answering either. So I go back to calling Jolene. "Ugh! Why doesn't anyone answer their phone!"

"What about my computer?" Vanessa asks.

"Right." I open her laptop and find the Lux file. "There are interview notes, pictures of the hotel, pictures of Earl Park, aerial pictures taken of the Handhoff tow yard. How'd you get those?"

"I used a drone. The thing is ... I don't think the Handhoffs killed anyone. It's not triggering anything. Shouldn't my mind be triggered?"

"It can. The first spirit I worked with, the one who gave me this car, he knew he'd been murdered but didn't know who killed him. As soon as we got close to figuring it out, it was like a gate opened, and all these memories came flooding back to him."

"How do I open the gate?"

I shrug. "Why don't you try taking everything out of your capsule and your receptacle and allow yourself to feel all the feelings and ..." I move my hands around helplessly, fishing for the right verbiage. "I don't know. Take a bath in them."

"Take a bath in my feelings?" she repeats, sounding skeptical.

"Yes," I say more confidently. "Take a bath in your feelings. It's called the ... Lane Immersion Method."

"It can't hurt." She wiggles around in her seat. "Okay. I need to bathe in my feelings ... it's not working, Lane."

"Let's talk about it. How do you feel about your breakup with Brian?"

"I feel upset. Betrayed, because I thought he was forever. We had plans. We even share a cellular plan! But who really meets their forever in college? I miss him. I'm ... heartbroken, but not as heartbroken as I thought I would be. I'm sad. I'm ... blah. I hate feeling my feelings."

"I know. I know. Don't stop," I say. "What about your dad? You found out that he is a criminal and Brian thinks he's the reason your grandma is dead."

"I'm mad about that. Of course. I mean ... I'm furious, actually. I'm *really* angry." She sounds surprised. "What an awful person. I will never forgive him. Not ever. He can be so arrogant, and he has this way about him, as if no one can ever touch him. I think I hate him. Wow. I really hate him. What a—" She spends the next two minutes dropping curse words I've never even heard of. And I read a lot of hot romance novels; there is some pretty creative cursing in those.

Vanessa is still going on when my phone pings with a text. It's from Tanner.

My mom doesn't know the name of the family that used to own the home, but she said Elvin Peterson ran it for many years. Do you want me to text him?

Also, my mom wants to know if you plan to put back all the flooring once you rid the house of all demons?

"Uh ... Vanessa?"

"Mother flippin' crap buckets!" She slaps her cheeks with trembling hands. "It's Elvin!"

"Did you read this text?" I hold up my phone.

"No. Zoe! You're a freaking genius. Your bathing method works. I remember! I remember! I remember!" She's punching the air. "I remember! I remember! I remember!"

"What happened?"

"I was having a really hard time controlling my emotions, and I made a rash decision to stop and get ice cream. Jolene called. Her voice was shaking, and she was talking so fast I could barely understand her. She said that Lux appeared to her in a dream last night and told her the person responsible for her death was Elvin Peterson. Jolene remembered that name. When she'd come to Fernn Valley to look for Lux, someone had told her there was a bed and breakfast and that Elvin ran it. She'd looked up Elvin and had gone to his work at the Trucker paper to talk to him, and he'd said that the bed and breakfast had closed down several years ago. I know he didn't say anything to her then about the Ishmaels still offering boarding, or she would have told me. Jolene said she'd had a bad vibe from Elvin back then, and she remembered him vividly. So when she had this dream, she thought it was Lux communicating with her. She woke up at two this morning and looked up this bed and breakfast in Fernn Valley. She found an old California trip forum from like ten years ago, and this woman said she'd stayed at the Fernn Valley Bed and Breakfast and that the manager was creepy and he had been looking through her window. It didn't say if she reported this or not, but it was enough for Jolene. She drove down to Trucker right then. She called me from outside the building as I was getting my ice cream. Her plan was to confront Elvin ... are you texting someone or writing down what I'm saying?"

I look up from my phone. "I'm texting Mike everything you're saying."

"Good. Where was I ... oh, got it. I'll admit, until I died, I did not believe in ghosts, or spirits, or an afterlife, or any of it. I figured that when you die, you die. You're no more. So of course I didn't believe Jolene had received a message from Lux. And I certainly didn't want her confronting this man who I thought was innocent of murder. Especially since he worked for a paper. I told Jolene to leave the building, go find a place to decompress because she was wound up. I told her I would talk to Elvin.

"I called the Trucker paper as soon as I hung up, and I was connected to Elvin, who was at his desk. I started by asking him a few warm-up questions. Like, did he go to the book festival? Does he know the Handhoffs? Because they were my prime suspects. He said that he covered the book festival for the paper and was there taking pictures. Then he said that he did know the Handhoffs. He'd gone to school with Gary. Then I asked him if he remembered seeing a gold hatchback with Oregon license plates at the festival, since he was taking pictures and it was a very ugly car. It stood out." She sits up straighter. "He replied with no, he hadn't seen any Civics with Oregon plates.

"I hadn't told him it was a Civic. That's when my radar went up. I immediately pounced. I asked him how he knew it was a Civic. Then I flooded him with questions like, did you hurt Lux? Where is her body? And I told him that I had information that linked him to the case, when obviously I didn't. I just hoped to get him flustered enough to slip again. That's what I was doing on my phone. I was attempting to record the conversation!"

My fingers are cramping from typing so fast. "Did he make another slip?"

"Yes! He did! He was flustered, and we were talking over each other. He told me I was ridiculous and he didn't have to listen to me. Then he mentioned something about the crawl space and how it was sealed, which didn't make any sense to me. I asked him what he meant then ...*bam*! I was at your house."

Dang. I'm tempted to copyright my immersion method.

I hit send on my text message to Mike. I'm about to call him when Vanessa's phone rings. I almost jump out of my seat I'm so on edge.

It's Jolene.

"What do I do?" I ask Vanessa.

"Answer!"

Solid plan. "Hello?"

"W-who is this?"

"Jolene, please listen to me. I am a good friend of Vanessa's, and I'm worried that you're in danger. Where are you?"

"I'm in Fernn Valley."

"Why? No. No. No. Please leave. Right now. Turn around and leave. Didn't you read my text messages?"

"I just saw them, but I don't understand what's going on. Who are you?"

"My name is Zoe Lane, and I am a friend of Vanessa's. We were investigating your daughter's case together."

"She has *never* mentioned your name," Jolene says. "Why do you have her phone?"

"Her dad gave me permission to grab her things from the coroner's office. Please, Jolene, listen to me. I need you to leave Fernn Valley."

"Coroner's office?" The puzzlement in her voice is like a splinter of ice in my heart. *Has she not heard?*

"Vanessa died this morning," I say.

For a moment she doesn't speak. I check to be sure we're still connected, and we are. I realize what a complete and total shock this much be, but I can't give her the proper amount of processing time. Not when the clock is ticking.

"She's ... dead? How?"

"Vanessa was in a car accident shortly after you talked to her. She immediately called the *Trucker Newspaper* after you guys hung up. She spoke to Elvin, and we're like ninety percent sure he's the killer."

"More like ninety-five," says Vanessa.

"Okay, we're ninety-five percent positive."

"You're telling me that Lux really *is* dead," says Jolene, and I feel horrible. I'm dumping terrible information on her in a hasty manner. "My momma gut told me she was alive until my dream, but hearing it out loud is ..."

I don't need to feel her feelings to know she's heartbroken. "Jolene, I know that I can give you peace and closure. All I need is for you to turn around and go to Trucker. I will follow you there, but we cannot be in Fernn Valley at the same time."

"I don't understand. I've been waiting all day for Vanessa to call me back, and finally I just gave up. I knew Elvin lived here, and I decided to find him myself since the police have been of zero help. I just stopped at the Food Mart to ask where Elvin lives, and I saw that Vanessa had called forty-seven times while I was driving."

"Listen to me, Jolene," I beg. "Please leave Fernn Valley."

"How do I know you're not working for Elvin?" she asks.

"I promise you that I'm not."

"Then how do you know so much about Elvin? Vanessa never mentioned you. Not once."

I look to Vanessa for help.

She fans her face. "I'm feeling a lot of emotions right now, and I'm having a very hard time thinking."

Great! "Then pull the plug on the tub and stuff everything back in a receptacle!"

"What was that?" Jolene asks.

My phone rings. It's Mike. I ask Jolene to hold on then I answer my cell.

"Jolene is here," I say instead of hello.

"And Elvin killed Lux?" he asks.

"We're ninety-five percent positive. Where are you?"

"I'm at the tow yard still. My Aunt Berthy couldn't find any information on a gold Honda Civic that came in within the last year. The fact that there's no paperwork means my uncle Gary didn't want anyone to know it was here. It doesn't mean he had anything to do with Lux's murder. It just means that someone paid him enough to dispose of the evidence. The man has no morals."

Agreed. Dang it! The dark spirit I felt at the accident likely was Gary, but it probably was Elvin too ... they were both there ...

Mother flippin' crap buckets! "Elvin was at the scene because he was on the phone with Vanessa when she crashed, and he wanted to make sure she was really dead. Otherwise he was probably going to take care of her death himself!" I am not even sure whom I'm saying this to. Probably Mike, since he's on the phone. Not Vanessa, since she's rocking in the fetal position, muttering something about being unable to pull the plug.

Okay, I'm vetoing the copyright idea.

"Hello ... hello!" I hear Jolene say, and I grab Vanessa's phone.

I have Mike in my left ear and Jolene in my right. "Jolene, listen to me, please. I will meet you in *Trucker* to go over everything."

"Zoe," Mike says. "I'm calling Sheriff Executer."

"No. Don't do that."

"Don't go to Trucker," says Jolene.

"No, yes. Yes. Yes. Yes. Go to Trucker."

"Okay, then I'll call him right now." Mike hangs up.

Gah. Obviously I suck at multitasking.

I take a cleansing breath and speak to Jolene. "The sheriff here is being notified. Please let him handle it and go to Trucker."

"Not a chance," Jolene says. "This is my girl, and I will not let her down. The police have done nothing for me. I don't know who you are or why you want me out of town. But I am sitting in the Food Mart parking lot looking at Elvin Peterson. He just pulled up. I will take matters into my own hands."

Click.

CHAPTER ELEVEN

"I cannot believe she just hung up on me!" I grab my phone, text Mike saying that Elvin is at the Food Mart, switch my car into sport mode, and am down the street three seconds later.

"Where are we going?" Vanessa asks.

"The Food Mart. Elvin and Jolene are there. Weren't you paying attention?"

"No! I was wallowing in the depths of despair. I hate the immersion method."

"Try meditating and stuffing all your feelings because things are about to get real heated, and I might need your zapping abilities."

Vanessa places her hands over her heart. "I can do this," she says, mostly to herself.

It takes us ten long, painful minutes to reach the Food Mart. The parking lot is packed, like every Fernn Valley resident has decided to go shopping at this exact moment.

"Look. There she is." Vanessa points to Jolene. It's the same woman from Mike's vision, and she's wearing the same outfit.

This is happening, I realize. Everything is falling right into place. The Food Mart is not far from the baseball fields. The sun is setting. Mike is wearing a clown shirt. Jolene is here in Fernn Valley. Brian can't be far. The only hope we have is to apprehend Elvin so he can't chase us into the forest and shoot Brian.

The good news is Jolene is yelling at Elvin, who is standing there completely speechless, holding an ice cream cone.

I come to a screeching stop and gasp. "Lux is with her."

Vanessa squints her eyes and leans forward, peering out the front window. "Well, I'll be damned. Who is with her?" she asks, referring to the spirit standing beside Lux. She's blonde and tan and has a butterfly tattoo on her ankle. It must be Brinkley/Britney.

Vanessa disappears and reappears beside Lux and Brinkley/Britney. The spirits all hug and start chatting. I put my car in park, stumble out, and run. Even though I'm in the middle of the lot, and there are quite a few cars that are now honking at me. Not that I care.

"Tell me what you did with my girl," Jolene is saying to Elvin. "Tell me!" She smacks the ice cream out of his hand.

The dark spirit I felt before grows stronger as I get closer to Elvin.

"I didn't do anything," Elvin says, and Vanessa shocks him.

He crumbles to the ground. And she shocks him again and again and again, chanting, "Tell the truth. Tell the truth. Tell the truth."

"Stop," I say and step closer to an incapacitated Elvin. I hate being around dark spirits. I hate having to feel their feelings and read their thoughts, but it's our best choice right now.

"He was covering the book festival for the paper when he saw Lux," I say, searching through his thoughts. His mind is a like a dark cave filled with previous revolting acts that I want to unsee as soon as they come to me. "He overheard Tanner tell her that his parents offered boarding. He knew the Ishmaels' house well. He'd spent many years there. That night, he tapped on her window to get her attention, and then he crawled under the home and into the closet. Like he'd done so many times before. Except Lux was different than the others. He'd always been able to get the women out of the house, where he'd strangle them. Lux fought back," I say, recoiling. "She fought hard, to the point he had no choice but to kill her right there before the Ishmaels woke up. He buried her body near the river, stripped her plates, and paid Gary Handhoff five hundred bucks to make the car disappear."

"That's where I am, too," says Brinkley/Britney. "My body is by the river."

"You are sick!" Vanessa shocks Elvin again, and he cries out in pain.

I go back to Elvin's thoughts. "Then Jolene showed up this morning. He saw her waiting outside in her car. She looked upset, and he assumed she'd figured it out. He was about to take care of her when Vanessa called. That's why he didn't kill Jolene. While on the phone with Vanessa, he heard a crash. He suspected Vanessa had been in a car accident, and he wanted to get there to grab her stuff before the cops did. But her body and belongings were already gone by the time he arrived."

It's not until I finish speaking that I notice the swarm of people that has formed around us. So many familiar faces. So many emotions emitting from the crowd. Fear, awe, skepticism, and confusion.

Mrs. Ishmael steps forward, holding a Drumstick. "Are you saying that he killed that girl in our home?"

"Yes. Just like he killed Lolly," I say, reading Elvin's thoughts. "He snuck in under the house, strangled her, and made it look like a suicide."

Mrs. Ishmael is engulfed in a jumble of relief and rage. She picks up a rock and throws it at Elvin, missing by a foot, but the sentiment is there.

Elvin can barely move. Probably because Vanessa is still shocking him over, and over, and over again. His body is convulsing with each shock. To everyone else, it looks like he's having a seizure.

A loud horn blares, and Sheriff E's (I can't say Executer, not after being in Elvin's head) SUV jumps the curb, and the crowd parts, allowing him through.

"There you are, Elvin," Sheriff E says. "I have questions for you."

"He just confessed." Jolene is in tears. "He admitted that he killed my baby. Well ... *she* admitted for him." She points to me, and my cheeks go red.

"I-I just sort of figured it out," I say. "He's a bad man. A bad, bad, bad man. A seriously bad—" I step away as to not be privy to his thoughts anymore because they are ... *bad*. Lolly, Brinkley/Britney, and Lux were not his only victims. He kills for fun.

Sheriff E pulls Elvin to his feet. He's sheet-white and dazed.

"Let's go have a little chat." Sheriff E escorts Elvin to the SUV, opens the back door, practically throws him in, gets behind the wheel, and backs up slowly.

I stand there frozen in shock, trying to make sense of what just happened, when Lux appears in front of me.

"You can see me, right?" she asks. Lux's spirit is even prettier than she was in Tanner's thoughts. Her hair is long and shiny. Her skin flawless, and her smile lights up her entire face. "I've been waiting for someone who can see me."

"This morning, I tried to reach you, but you wouldn't come," I say.

"I didn't know it was you. I felt something pulling me, but I had to stay with my mom. She was in Trucker waiting for Vanessa to call back. I was so worried she was going to confront

Elvin. Believe me, when I came to her in her dream, I did not think she was going to leave in the middle of the night."

"Why didn't you tell her sooner?" I ask.

"Because I didn't know. I couldn't remember anything. She told me." Lux grabs Brinkley/Britney's hand. Until this moment, I had no idea spirits could touch each other. Makes sense.

"Zoe!" Mike yells. He's pushing through the crowd. "Zoe!" He scoops me up off the ground and spins me around.

"We got him," I say.

"I know." Mike lowers me to the ground.

I take a deep breath for what feels like the first time all day. "Can you feel Lux?"

"I can now ... is there someone else here with her?"

"Yes." I turn to Brinkley/Britney. "What *is* your name?"

"Brintley."

Oh. Mrs. Ishmael was close-ish.

"Brintley is here," I say.

"What are you talking about?" Jolene asks. "Who is Brintley? And you said Lux is here? She's here with me?"

"She is," I say. "She's with another one of Elvin's victims, Brintley."

Brintley steps forward. "I remembered everything that happened to me. For the last year, I've been searching for another one of Elvin's victims who hadn't transitioned yet. Someone who could help me put that creep behind bars."

Lux places a loving hand on her mother's cheek. "Tell her that I haven't left her side since I died. Tell her I'm the one who blows her wind chimes in the morning."

"Lux is here," I say to Jolene. "She has not left your side since she died, and she makes sure the wind chimes outside of your window chime every day as soon as you wake up. It's her way of saying good morning."

"I know," says Jolene, tears spilling out of her eyes.

"I'm ready." Lux kisses her mother on the cheek then says good-bye to Vanessa. "Thank you for everything," she says. "I'm sorry you died."

Vanessa waves her hands as if to say *no big deal.*

Lux gives Brintley a hug, and the two fade away.

"They're gone, right?" Mike asks.

"They are."

I turn to Vanessa.

"I don't know why you're looking at me," she says. "I'm not transitioning anywhere. I just caught a serial killer, and we're going to write about it." Vanessa taps the tips of her fingers together almost gleefully. "It's going to be big!"

That's right. The article. She also needs to make peace with Brian before she can go anywhere. Speaking of Brian.

Speaking of Brian ...

"We're good, right? We fixed it." I ask Mike and do a quick survey of our surrounding area. "We're not far from the softball field, and we're all together. The sun has set. The killer has been caught, though. And we're at the Food Mart. Not in the forest. We're good."

Mike starts to nod his head then stops and says, "No."

"What are you talking about?" asks Jolene.

"I would recognize Elvin," Mike says as if just realizing, "even if he was covered in mud. The guy that is going to kill Brian is way bigger than him."

"How can we not be good?" Vanessa is in Mike's face. "Are you broken?" She shocks him, and he falls to the ground.

"Okay, that was not necessary," I say and help Mike up. "No! Your nose is bleeding!"

Mike touches his face and marvels down at the blood. He looks exactly like he does in his vision.

"That's her!" I hear someone yell out. "Zoe Lane is right over there!"

We all swivel around.

A man with eyebrows as thick as my arms, a shaved head, and five o'clock shadow pushes through the crowd. He's wearing slim black pants, a tight white shirt, and a black revolver is clutched in his hand.

"What is my dad doing here?" Vanessa says.

Her dad?

The man is tall with a strong jaw and built like a brick wall. "Are you Zoe Lane?" he asks.

I want to say no. So I do. "No. Not Zoe."

"Hey, Zoe," says Dominick, coming out of the Food Mart. "What's going on around here?"

"You *are* Zoe." Max's chest is rising and falling at a rapid pace.

Okay, so here's what I know about Vanessa's dad, Max: He's big and scary and, based on his thoughts, he believes I am the one responsible for his daughter's death. It was the faux fur. As soon as I said it, he was convinced it was a message from his daughter. I'd kidnapped Vanessa, got the information I needed, and then called to blackmail him. Which is why he agreed to let me have her stuff. Vanessa's phone has a LoJack on it. He knew he'd be able to find me.

Also, I know no matter what I say or what I do, he has already decided that I'm dead.

Time to run.

I take off into the forest. Mike and Jolene are following. "Shock him!" I scream. "Shock him!"

"I'm trying," Vanessa cries. "He's not responding."

"Try harder!"

I jump over a bush and zigzag through the trees.

A shot is fired. Then another. And another. Followed by an explosion. I look up at the fireworks filling the sky. This is all happening. There is no stopping it now.

I check over my shoulder to see if Brian is here. I don't see him. Not yet.

I'll take the bullet, I decide. No matter what happens. I will take the bullet. Max is after me. I'm the one he wants dead. Death won't be that bad. I'll have Mike help me say good-bye to my parents. Then I'll transition and go hang out with Lolly. She seems like good people.

Not sure why I'm still running.

But I am. Until I slip and fall to my hands and knees. When I stand, I take note of the mud coating my pants. Mike grabs my arm and tells me to hurry, but I don't move.

"It doesn't matter," I say and look around. "This is the spot. Please listen for me when I'm gone."

"What are you talking about? You're not dying."

"Yes, I will die instead of Brian."

"Who is that crazy man?" Jolene asks in a panic. "Why are we running? What is happening?"

"It's Vanessa's father. I sort of blackmailed him earlier. Long story. Anyway. He thinks I killed Vanessa."

"Tell him you didn't!" Jolene is near hysterics.

I can hear Max approaching, and my stomach clenches in nerves. This is it.

"No!" Jolene jumps in front of me. "You gave me peace. I will not let him touch you. I'd rather go."

"No. I'm not letting you." I step in front of her.

Then Mike steps in front of us both. "Stay back," he says.

So I step in front of him.

Jolene in front me.

Mike in front of us both.

We do this for a while until Max barrels through the trees and stops. The fireworks are still going off overhead, and the flash from the explosions brightens his face. He must have slipped along the way because his face and hands are covered in mud.

"Your daughter's death was an accident," Mike says. "She ran off the road while she was on the phone."

"Not buying it. She"—he points the end of his revolver at me —"knew information only Vanessa would. You kill my kid, I kill you."

A commotion in the bushes grabs his attention before he can pull the trigger. I shove Jolene out of the way. Mike grabs my arm to keep me from confronting Max. I kick and thrash and spit and beg.

Brian jumps out from behind a bush.

"No!" I scream. "Brian, go away."

"Brian," Max practically spits out the words. "I should have known you had something to do with this."

"No. I didn't. Neither did Zoe. I just got back from the AT&T store in Trucker, and I was able to get Vanessa's cell records since we shared an account. She was on the phone with the Trucker paper when the crash happened. I called the editor there, who put me in contact with the secretary, who told me that Vanessa was talking to Elvin. Elvin used to manage the bed and breakfast until the bank seized the house, and then it was sold to the Ishmaels, who now do boarding. Vanessa was investigating the disappearance of Lux, and I think she'd figured out it was Elvin, which is why she contacted him, was distracted while driving, and ran into the welcome sign."

Well, I'll be damned.

Vanessa throws her hands up in the air. "Why couldn't you have put that brain to good work and help me in the first place?"

Max is shaking his head. "Nice try." He fires two shots so fast neither Mike nor Jolene nor I can move in time.

Then, just like it was supposed to happen, Brian goes down.

CHAPTER TWELVE

I've spent a lot of time around death. Investigating murders. Looking for missing people. Helping spirits transition to the next phase of their existence. I've been around spirits moments after they died. What I have not experienced is being around someone who is actively dying.

And I don't intend to start now.

I have my hands on Brian's stomach in an attempt to stop the bleeding while screaming at Vanessa to, "Shock your dad!"

As soon as Brian hit the ground, Mike charged Max and was able to get him off balance. The two men are rolling around on the forest floor.

Jolene places her hands over mine. "Apply as much pressure as possible," she says, and I catch her thoughts. She worked as an ER nurse for fifteen years. She knows from experience this doesn't look good.

I have *zero* experience in the medical field, and even I know a gunshot to the gut isn't good.

"Shock him!" I'm screaming at Vanessa.

"I can't!" She's standing over the two men. Mike is on top of Max, pinning Max's arms down. Then Max is on Mike with his hands firmly around Mike's neck. Then Mike is on Max, and Max is on Mike, and Mike is on Max. They're blurring into one giant roll of testosterone. "I don't want to accidentally touch Mike. If he goes down, my dad will get the upper hand and kill him."

Oh, for heaven's sake! If I had a time machine, I would go back to the moment "blackmail" exited Vanessa's mouth and shoot the idea down. Except, we wouldn't have been able to get her phone, which wouldn't have sparked her memory, which wouldn't have resulted in Elvin being taken into custody, which will ultimately save lives.

That is, unless we'd had ten dollars!

"Get the gun," Brian rasps, his lips alarmingly white. "Find ... the gun." He moans and tries to sit up. I urge him to be still and frantically survey the forest floor, which is covered in pine needles.

"I'll find it." Jolene presses down harder. "Continue to apply as much pressure as you can." She turns and crawls on the ground, sweeping her hands around until she finds the gun.

Oh, good. At least no one else should get shot.

"Vanessa! Just shock whomever," I say. "Jolene has the gun!"

Vanessa's mouth goes to a determined line, and she slaps the two men. Mike lets out a cry, but Max is not nearly as phased. So Vanessa shocks him again, and again, and again, until he's on his back, looking up at the fireworks.

"Did you say Vanessa?" Brian asks, his voice so hoarse I have to put my ear to his mouth. "Why did you say Vanessa?"

Oh, my. I stare into Brian's beautiful gray eyes. Tears clog the back of my throat, and I choke down a sob. I knew I'd have to tell Brian about my gifts one day. I'd played out different scenarios in my mind. Scenario one: I'd sit down and tell him the truth about my gifts. He'd take off his shirt and whisk me to bed. Scenario two: I'd stand up and tell him the truth about my gifts. He'd rip off his shirt and whisk me to bed. Scenario three: I'd lie down and tell him the truth about my gifts. He'd peel off his shirt and whisk me to bed. Basically all scenarios ended with a shirtless Brian. *None* of them involved a gunshot wound.

But this might be my only chance to tell him. "I'm a medium," I say. "That's how I knew all about Willie MacIntosh, and Penelope, and Drew. Mike is also a medium, and he can see glimpses of the future." A tear trickles down my cheek. "I knew you were going to kiss me before you even showed up this morning."

Brian's breathing is labored, and his eyelids begin to close.

"No. No. No," I say and press down harder on his wound.

"Brian Windsor, you are not going to die!" Vanessa drops to her knees. "Do you understand me?" She touches Brian's shoulder. He violently jerks, and his eyes become wide as saucers.

There's a cacophony of voices approaching, and I look up. Sheriff E steps from behind a tree with his gun drawn. He's followed by two men in police uniforms. Both have their weapons out and ready to shoot. It doesn't take long for them to assess the situation.

Jolene has Max's revolver pointed at Max's chest, while Mike is struggling to his feet.

One officer goes right to Jolene and pries the gun from her shaky hands, while the other tends to Mike. The sheriff is down on the ground beside me, talking to the radio attached to his shoulder, calling for a medic while he mentally prepares his resignation letter.

"He was shot," I say, as if it weren't obvious.

Sheriff E pulls a pair of gloves from his belt and slaps them on. "Let me take over." He replaces my hands with his and tells Brian to hang on.

I scoot back and hug my knees to my chest while I watch the sheriff and Jolene tend to him.

Eventually the fireworks stop and the paramedics arrive. Brian is still alive when they load him into the back of the rig. But I have no idea for how long. I feel better knowing that Jolene is with him. She decided to ride along, wanting to put her nursing skills to use.

We're standing in the parking lot of the Food Mart, surrounded by emergency vehicles and concerned patrons. Mike uses me as a crutch, as he's still recovering from his fight with built-like-a-brick Max and his shock from Vanessa. It is interesting how she only has the ability to incapacitate men and not women with her powers. Or maybe women are just stronger.

Probably the latter.

"There's my dad," Vanessa says when a young officer steps out from the shadows of the forest, escorting Max, whose hands are cuffed behind his back. Despite the fact that he did shoot Brian, and he killed Vanessa's grandma, and he came all this way to murder me, I do feel a *little* sorry for the man. I can't help myself. He lost his daughter today.

"Wait here," I tell Mike and approach Max. "I meant what I said on the phone about Vanessa. I do see her—"

"Don't," Vanessa cuts me off, appearing at her father's side. "Don't tell him that I love him regardless. Tell him that I forget him."

"Don't you mean forgive?" I ask.

"No, tell him that I forget him. I have chosen to forget him not because he deserves to be forgotten, but because I deserve to have peace."

I'm fairly certain that is not how the saying goes, but she's the self-help expert. "Vanessa has chosen to forget you," I say.

Max's eyes are so sad and vacant it tugs on my heartstrings.

Until Vanessa yells, "Stop that!" into my ear. "I can see it on your face, Zoe Lane. Do not feel sorry for that man. Not for one second."

Okay. *Okay*.

Max's escorting officer puts him in the back of his squad car and takes off.

"I'm going with Brian," Vanessa decides. "I can do that, right?"

"I don't see why not."

She starts to leave then abruptly turns around. "Why didn't I go find Brian myself today and then tell you where he was?"

Uh ... Mike and I exchange a look. That would have been a good idea, actually. I've had spirits who can't leave my side, and I've had spirits who can come and go as they please. It hadn't occurred to me to see which category Vanessa fell into.

"Oh, for heaven's sake." She rolls her eyes before she disappears.

Guess it's the latter.

"Do you want to follow them to the hospital?" Mike asks.

I shake my head and wipe a tear spilling down my cheek. "I'll talk to him after he dies."

Mike tilts his head. "He doesn't die."

"What?"

"Brian doesn't die."

"What?"

"Brian doesn't die."

"What?"

"Brian ... Windsor ... does ... not ... die," he says.

"I-I ... what?"

"It came to me about an hour ago."

"What?"

"I was racing here when I caught a glimpse of Brian awake in a hospital bed."

I'm so overcome with relief that it feels like my chest has

been pumped full of helium and I might float away. He's going to live. Brian Windsor is going to—hold on. "Where is Elvin?" I suddenly realize that Sheriff E's SUV is parked next to my car, and his back seat is empty. He couldn't have had time to drop Elvin off at the station before he returned to the scene.

"Another police officer must have taken him," says Mike.

"Are we sure? Because Sheriff E doesn't look too happy."

Mike turns around to see for himself.

The sheriff approaches his vehicle cautiously with his gun drawn. He has the same expression my dad has when he accidentally leaves the back door open and Jabba gets out. Though Jabba is lazy and ornery and never gets far. Elvin is gritty and vile and a serial killer!

Sheriff E shoves his gun into the holster and radios for backup saying, "Officer down."

Officer down?

Mike and I rush to the other side of the SUV and find a young deputy on his hands and knees, struggling to catch his breath. The passenger side door is wide open, and Elvin is nowhere to be seen.

"How did this happen?" I demand.

Sheriff E is tending to the young deputy, helping him to a sitting position. "Have you been shot?" he asks.

The young man shakes his head and struggles to get words out. Not that he has to.

I already know from his thoughts Elvin strangled the deputy put in charge to watch him.

"Why didn't you handcuff Elvin?" I demand. "How could you let this happen!" I know I said I wouldn't tell the new sheriff how to do his job, or pick apart his investigations, but honestly. "You let him go!" I'm hysterical, but that's only because Brian almost lost his life catching Elvin, and now he's gone.

Sheriff E doesn't respond, instead he radios for more

backup, for search dogs, and helicopters, and for a whole bunch of resources that Fernn Valley doesn't have and is forced to borrow from the neighboring county.

The deputy is taken to the hospital, and Sheriff E sets up a base camp in the Food Mart parking lot. Mike and I sit on the hood of his Jeep and wait, and wait, and wait, eager to hear, "we've got him!" But the words never come.

It's around six in the morning when Mike and I concede defeat. We can no longer stay awake, Sheriff E is not ready to stop, and they're still combing the forest with the search dogs brought in from Trucker County.

A quick power nap in the front seats of my car, and Mike and I are on our way to see Brian at the Trucker Hospital. Fernn Valley only has Dr. Karman's office—and his remedy for everything is 800 mg of Motrin. Brian's injuries are beyond ibuprofen.

Vanessa had returned around midnight to tell us that he was out of surgery and stable. She vanished before we could tell her about Elvin. I have no idea how she'll take the news.

It's a long car ride to Trucker and a fight to stay awake. Knowing Brian will live is the only thing keeping me going. I turn into the underground parking structure at the hospital, pull into a space away from all other cars on the third level because, "the i8 deserves respect," according to Mike.

We take the elevator up to the lobby in silence. My head feels as if it's stuffed with cotton, and my eyelids are too heavy to open all the way. Mike and I must look as good as we feel, because the nurse working the information desk hesitates at first to tell us Brian's room number, giving us the once over.

"Room two twenty-three," she finally says. I can hear the *pssshhhhhh* of an aerosol can as soon as we walk away, and I check over my shoulder to see the nurse disinfecting everything Mike and I touched. Not that I blame her. I'm still rocking my newly released inmate sweatpants and shirt, which are covered in blood and mud. Mike has on the clown shirt, and his face is streaked in dirt and dried blood. We look like the walking dead.

Actually, scratch that. I've seen the walking dead. We look *way* worse.

The hospital isn't busy, and we go down a hall and find the elevator. Mike presses the call button. "Do you think Brian remembers everything about you being a medium?"

"If he doesn't, then I'm going to tell him the truth."

"How do you think he'll react?"

"I don't know. He's just been shot, and his ex-girlfriend is dead. Me seeing dead people might not seem like that big of a deal."

Mike shoves his hands into the front pockets of his pants and watches the numbers on top of the elevator. "It's pretty crazy to think about how quickly the future can be altered. If Vanessa hadn't called Elvin, she would be alive. Jolene would be dead. Brian wouldn't have been shot."

True. My mind goes back to Elvin out there running loose, doing who knows what to who knows whom. His thoughts were so awful I might never sleep again. He has to be stopped.

"You don't have any visions of the future yet?" I've asked him this about a thousand times since Elvin escaped. Each time he reminds me these are gifts not powers, and they don't always work as we want.

"No, I haven't." There's an angst to his voice that wasn't there before, and he omits the *gifts aren't powers* spiel.

Has he had a vision? Does he not want to tell me because the outcome is not good? Or is he just overly exhausted? Or is it all three? I shuffle closer, hoping to get a better sense of his feelings. I too am overly exhausted, and my brain isn't quite as sharp.

Mike is tired, of course. He's sore, of course. He's anxious about Elvin, but he's also anxious about being here, about me seeing Brian because ... *Oh, my.*

"I love you," Mike says, still watching the numbers.

I gulp and tuck a strand of hair behind my ear. "I know."

"I know you know."

"I know you know I know," I say and smile up at him.

"I'm not Mr. Rogers. But I get you in a way that no one else will."

"I know."

The elevator doors part, and we ride up to the second floor without uttering a word. I've never had anyone that I wasn't related to say I love you. It feels good. And scary. And confusing.

Jolene is in the waiting room, sitting by herself in front of the fish tank.

"I should go wait with her," Mike says.

"She shouldn't be alone right now," I agree.

"Does she know Elvin escaped?" Mike asks.

"I can't tell from this far away, but you should probably tell her what happened."

"She's not going to take the news well."

"Is that an opinion or a vision?"

"It's an obvious prediction." He swipes a strand of hair from my forehead and tilts my chin, forcing me to look him in the eyes. "Remember what I said."

"I will," I promise and walk away.

The problem is that from the moment I picked up *The Gazette* and saw Brian's picture printed under the headline *New Editor in Chief*, I've loved him. Well, maybe not *loved*. I was infatuated. My infatuation grew to a crush. My crush morphed into stronger feelings, and when I knew Brian was going to die, the thought of living in this world without him was unbearable.

Mike is fun, and understanding, and handsome, and easy to be around. He gets me in a way that no one else could. I'm honored that he loves me.

But he's not Brian.

Love triangles are the single most overused trope in every hot romance novel I've read. Even though they're incredibly frustrating, I love them. I love guessing whom the heroine will end up with. I love the back and forth. I love picking a team.

I do not, however, love living one.

It's not quite as exhilarating as the *Real Hot Househusbands of Oklahoma* made it out to be. Not even a little bit.

Brian is asleep when I enter the room, and Vanessa is at the window, looking out at the construction happening next door.

"They're renovating the pediatric cancer wing," she says without moving.

"It's now the Willie MacIntosh Center for Pediatric Cancer Treatment."

"Willie MacIntosh was the first dead guy you helped, right?"

"He was."

"I remember that," she says. "Brian was supposed to come up to Portland for a visit but cancelled. He said he was working on a story about a millionaire who had possibly been murdered. It was the second time he had cancelled a visit. I could feel he was slipping away. That's one of the reasons the Lux case was perfect. I thought Brian and I would work together and reconnect. But he didn't want to do the story. Now I know why. It wasn't about Lux at all. It was him distancing himself from my family and me."

"Are you ready to speak to Brian?" I ask.

"I have to. It's part of my five-step transition plan. Step one: make peace with Brian. Step two: write the article. Step three: submit to the *Oregon Times*. Step three: say good-bye to you and Mike. Step five: transition ... why aren't you writing this down?"

I suspect the news of Elvin's escape will add a lot more steps to her five-step transition plan. I really don't want to tell her, but she has to know.

"Zoe?" comes Brian's hoarse voice. "Is that you?"

"It is." I move forward and grab Brian's hand. He looks so pale and tired I feel bad that I woke him.

"I thought he was going to kill you," he says.

"If you're talking about Vanessa's dad, then yes, he was going to kill me."

"When I was driving back from Trucker, he passed me in his Ferrari." Brian licks his chapped lips and tries to sit up before I stop him. "When I saw the commotion at the Food Mart, I stopped, and everyone said you were being chased by a man with a gun. I put two and two together." He gives my hand a squeeze. "I remember what you said."

"About spirits?"

"Mmhmm. I've known for a while."

"No, you have not," Vanessa says. "Sure, maybe he figured it out today, but he hasn't known for *a while*." She hooks her fingers into air quotes. "Last month, he gave me the hardest time when I went to a palm reader in Florida. Even if it was only for fun, and a total sham since the psychic said I was destined to have a long life. *Pfft*. I should get my money back."

I suck in my bottom lip to hide a smile. To think twenty-four hours ago, I couldn't even say Vanessa's name without breaking it into syllables. The mere thought of her sparked jealousy, insecurity, and annoyance. I wanted her to go away.

Now?

I'm dreading having to say good-bye.

But I have to.

It's part of her plan.

"Brian," I say. "Vanessa is here, and she needs closure before she can go."

Brian wrinkles his brow. This is hard for him. Paranormal anything is so far out of his comfort level he might as well be on another planet.

Vanessa appears at the side of his bed. With a roll of her shoulders, she clasps her hands over her heart. "Tell him to get a new hairstyle. The side comb is way too dated."

I give her a look.

"What? This is my good-bye, and that's what I want him to know."

Fine. "Brian, Vanessa would like you to explore different hairstyle options."

"That sounds like her," he says with a strained laugh.

"Good." Vanessa takes a seat in the chair and crosses her legs. "Now, how does this work? Do I have to say something, and then he says something? Or can I just sit here, and you can read my mind?"

"Whatever you're comfortable with," I say.

"I'm comfortable with you. Get in my head, Lane." She wiggles around in the seat. "I am bathing in my emotions." She leans her head back and closes her eyes. "Go for it."

Right. Okay. I shift my focus to Brian, who has the most perplexed expression on his face. "Vanessa didn't mean anything she said yesterday," I start. "She's not upset with you. You've always treated her with love and respect, and she will cherish your time together always. She wishes for you to take a few more risks, and for heaven's sake, please throw away the Oregon State shirt that you wear to bed *every* night. It's old, and it's faded, and it has a bleach stain on the sleeve. It's not attractive, and it must go." I give Vanessa a look.

"Trust me," she says. "I'm doing you a favor. It's hideous."

Oh, geez. I roll my shoulders, blow out a breath, and keep going. "She wants you to know that she'll always love you."

Brian is quietly studying the foot of the bed. "Tell her that

I'm sorry, and that I'll always remember her." He's holding back for a number of reasons. Most of which are that he is currently lying in a hospital bed, with his dead ex-girlfriend on one side and the woman he likes on the other side, a woman who is telling him what his dead ex-girlfriend is saying. It's a little too weird for Brian.

Lucky for him, I can read his feelings. "Brian wants you to know that you're the strongest person he's ever met. He loves you. He respects you. He isn't sure he can throw away the shirt, but he'll put it in his bottom drawer. He's going to miss you terribly. He blames himself for your death. No matter what you say, he'll always wonder if he'd helped with the Lux case if you'd still be alive."

Brain gasps. "How'd you know all that?"

Oh, right. I tap my forehead as if to say *d'oh.* "I can also feel other people's feelings, and I can read their thoughts. I'm getting pretty dang good at it, too." If I do say so myself.

"Hells yeah you are." Vanessa raises her hand, and we give each other an air high five.

"Did you just give Vanessa a high five?" Brian sounds so completely freaked out that I can't help but laugh.

"No, I didn't give her a high five because she has the ability to shock people."

Brian shakes his head and now Vanessa is laughing. "Oh, Bri, I'm going to miss you." She blows him a kiss and stands up straight. "I'm ready for step two. You still have my laptop in your car, right? Let's get typing."

"There's just one more step that you might want to add."

"I already told you, I *forgot* my dad. I feel good about it. I'm good."

"No, step three should be find Elvin."

"I already did."

"Well, he sort of escaped."

"He got away!" Vanessa explodes. "How did he get away? He was in the back of the sheriff's car when I last saw him."

"Well, he strangled the deputy in charge of watching him and managed to escape. We have no idea where he is."

"I'm going to find him." She's doing that determined pace thing while biting at her nails that she did when we first met. "He is not getting away with murder. Not on my watch. I'll see you two later."

And *poof*, she's gone.

"What happened?" Brian asks.

"Vanessa left."

"Did she go to heaven?"

"No."

"Oh. Got it. Hell?"

"No! She didn't go to hell. Didn't you hear what I just said? Elvin escaped."

"I am on *a lot* of morphine, and my brain is having a hard time keeping up. Elvin isn't in custody?"

"No, and Vanessa is looking for him."

"Vanessa Tobin is after him?" Brian's mouth twitches into a smile. "I almost feel sorry for the guy."

"I'm going to let you rest, okay." I start to pull my hand back, but Brian won't let go.

"Are you really with Mike Handhoff, or are you two just partners?" he asks.

"We're partners."

"Good." He pulls me down and cups my cheek. His hand feels warm against my skin, and he still smells of orange zest and fall leaves with a little bit of antiseptic thrown in. I lower my lids and lean in. Our lips meet. It's a fleeting peck but enough to confirm my feelings.

CHAPTER THIRTEEN

Mike and Jolene are in the waiting room watching the fish tank. The news station is on in the background. Elvin's face fills the screen. They still haven't found him. At least it'll be harder for him to hide now.

"Do you need a place to stay tonight?" I ask Jolene. She looks beat.

"I've already had a lot of offers," she says.

"From whom?"

"Them," says Mike, and he gestures to the room. I hadn't noticed. On the other side of the fish tank sit a row of familiar faces. Mr. and Mrs. Clark, Mr. and Mrs. Ishmael, Mr. and Mrs. Batch, and sitting in the last two seats are my parents.

Mom rushes to give me a hug. Her familiar Aqua Net scent is both soothing and suffocating. "Zoe, sweetie, you look terrible."

"I know, Mom." I also know she doesn't mean it in a bad, nagging, mother-type of way. She means it as the honest-to-goodness truth.

"You okay?" My dad gives my arm a squeeze. He looks like

Tom Selleck but acts like Mr. Rogers. Which makes me think of Brian ...

Huh.

"I really want a bath and a bed." I cover a yawn. "What about you?" I ask Mike.

"Sure, I could use your bath and bed as well." He winks.

Oh, geez.

No one wants to leave Brian alone. His parents are coming down from Portland and aren't due here until tonight, so we decide to stay with him in shifts.

Mr. and Mrs. Batch take the first shift, and the rest of us caravan home. My parents lead the way in our van, which has their picture plastered on the side. It's my dad giving my mom a piggyback ride. *We're in your Lane* is printed on the bottom along with their real estate license. It's tacky, yet effective.

By the time we get home, I can barely keep my eyes open. I pull into the garage and plug my car in. Mike touches the *bith* etched on the passenger side door. "I can buff all the scratches out. They're not too deep."

"Really?"

"Mmmhmmm. I'll do it for a small price." He winks.

"Like nothing? Cause that's about all I can afford."

"You're in luck. That's about all I charge."

I walk around my car and squeeze between the bumper and garage door. It's a *tight* fit.

Mike tenses as I approach. "I'm not apologizing for how I feel or what I told you."

"I didn't ask you to."

"You have that *I have bad news for you* look on your face."

"I wasn't going to say anything about what you said. You

confused my *bad news* face with my *get me in bed* face," I say. "But since we're on the subject. You barely know me. How can you say you love me?"

"Because I do." He traces my jawline with his finger, sending a brigade of goose bumps down my arms. "I've spent my entire life pretending to be something that I'm not. Every friend I've had, girl I've dated, they all thought they knew me, but they didn't. I've felt more myself being around you than I ever have. And I know it's not just because you're a medium and you have these gifts that are better than mine. Trust me, it would be easier to be with a girl who can't read my thoughts. I love you for *you*. All of you. To be honest, I've had a crush on you for years. You just didn't know it."

"I didn't. How did I not know? Can you hide your feelings from me?" I give him a playful nudge.

"Uhhh, I don't know. Maybe." He clenches his jaw and a small vein over his right eye pops out. "What am I feeling right now?"

I concentrate ... I see ... I see ... nothing! There's nothing there! Oh, how sweet the silence is. It's exhausting knowing what is going through everyone's head at all times.

"You have a constipated face on when you're hiding your thoughts," I say. "But it works."

Mike relaxes, and his feelings return.

"The thing is, Mike," I say, wringing my hands.

"Nothing good comes after, 'The thing is, Mike.'"

I laugh. "The *thing* is ... wait." I catch a hint of a dark spirit.

"Lay it on me, Lane. I can handle rejection—"

I slap my hand over his mouth. "I think he's here," I whisper. "I can feel his spirit."

Mike's eyes go distant, and I know that face. It's his *I'm seeing the future* face. "He came for you, but your parents got home first. He's here in your parents' room. You're going to attack him with a hammer."

"Does he die? Do I die? Does anyone die?"

"I don't know. The vision is really, really foggy."

"Crap!" I turn the doorknob. It's locked, and I don't have my key. No. No. No. I'm rifling through my dad's toolbox and pull out a hammer, when Mike kicks open the door.

That works, too.

"I'm here!" I call out. I still have my dad's hammer clutched in my hands. The grandfather clock in the living room chimes twelve times, muting my cries. I tiptoe down the hallway. Elvin's spirit grows stronger and stronger, and I peek into my parents' room.

Elvin is standing at the foot of the bed with a gun pressed against my mother's temple. My dad is standing by the closet, the safe he keeps on the top shelf is wide open, and his gun is positioned in his hands and aimed at Elvin. Jabba is on the bed, napping.

I start to move, and Mike holds me back. *Wait*, he mouths. *You're not going to end this situation with a hammer*. He slips his phone from his pocket.

Who are you texting? I mouth.

Sheriff E, he mouths back.

That's great and all, but I can't just stand here and do nothing if my mother is going to die!

"I'm here," I announce and enter the room with my hammer.

My mom shakes her head. "No, Zoe. Don't."

"It's me you want." I drop the hammer and put my hands in the air. "Let her go and take me."

A Cheshire cat smile spreads across his face. "I'll take both of you." In one sweeping gesture he wraps my mom in a choke hold and points the gun at me.

"Leave her alone, or I'll shoot," my dad says. I don't think I've ever heard my dad raise his voice before.

"Stop!" Mike is in the doorway, pointing his cell phone at us.

Elvin snickers. "Are you going to hurt me with your phone?"

"No. You're on Instagram live right now. Everything you do from this moment forward will be broadcasted to thousands of people. There will be no denying it."

Mike's idea is brilliant ... if we were dealing with your average criminal. Elvin finds the idea of killing my mother and me live on the Internet to be exhilarating. What a wacko.

"Hello, world," Elvin almost sings. "I'm your not-so-friendly neighbor k—" He collapses to the floor. The gun drops and fires, sending a bullet through the drywall.

Vanessa is hovering over Elvin. "I knew I'd find you." She shocks him again, and again, and again.

"Is he having a seizure?" my mom asks in horror.

"Something like that."

Jabba leaps off the bed and hisses at Vanessa, who continues to shock Elvin until he's rendered unconscious. "That'll teach you to mess with Vanessa Tobin."

Dad runs over and ushers my mother and me out the door, grabbing Elvin's gun along the way. Mike stands there in the hallway with his mouth hanging open.

"Did you really get that on Instagram?" I ask.

"No, your house has sucky reception. Is he dead?"

"Not yet." Vanessa smacks Elvin across the face with all her might.

That might have done it.

CHAPTER FOURTEEN

Or not.

Within minutes, emergency vehicles surround our house. This is the most work any of Fernn Valley's first responders have ever had to do in a single twenty-four hours.

Elvin is barely alive and taken by ambulance to Trucker Hospital. Mom and Dad are barely lucid, so freaked out by the ordeal of walking in to find a serial killer waiting for them. I am barely awake, so exhausted from a full day of crime fighting.

I rest my head on Mike's shoulder. We're sitting on the curb across the street from my house, watching Sheriff E interview my parents.

"Do all your cases end like this?" Mike asks.

"Not quite. They're never easy, though."

"Step two complete!" Vanessa announces, doing a triumphant fist pump. "Step three, write the article. I'll get started. Is your room the one that's painted pink with the doll collection?"

"Yes," I say reluctantly.

"Cool. I'll meet you there when you're ready. Bring my

laptop." She fades away so quickly I don't even have time to say anything.

"Did she just leave?" Mike asks.

"Yes, she did. I need to help her with her article."

"I heard. So, remember when we were in your garage, and you were about to let me down then this crazy guy with a gun showed up, and we all almost died?"

"Sounds familiar."

"I am ready now."

"I'm *so* tired, and I'm going to see Brian at five. Can I let you down tomorrow?"

"What if a spirit shows up tomorrow?"

I drop my head into my hands. "Please tell me that's a joke, not a vision. I need at least three days to recover."

"It's a joke, Lane."

I peek up at him. "Better be. By the way, where are you going to stay now?"

"Definitely not staying at the Ishmaels. I suspect no one will for quite some time. I think I'll hit up the Fernn Valley Hotel until your parents can find me a place to live."

"Do they know you're looking for a house?"

"Not yet. I'll talk to them when things have settled."

We do a collective sigh, and I stretch my arms out in front of me. "I guess I'll let you down now. Just to get it over with," I say.

"Sounds good." He wiggles around until we're facing each other. "Go ahead."

"You said you had friends and girlfriends who didn't really know *you*. That's not my story. I don't pretend around my friends, because I don't have friends. My parents sheltered me my entire life. There were no parties. No sleepovers. No boyfriends. No high school dances. I've never been in a relationship with anyone. Platonic or romantic. Everything I know about love and dating comes from books. Up until a few months ago, I didn't even have a driver's license. I didn't even know who *I* was. But now I do. I've liked Brian for *so* long, and he wants to be with *me*. Even after I told him about my gifts."

Mike is studying the asphalt.

"I don't know what the future holds ... well, unless you tell me," I say with a smile. "But, what I do know is that right now, I want to give a relationship a try. And I want to try it with you."

Mike makes a strangled sound and whips his head around. "What?"

"I want you."

"What?"

"I want you."

"What?"

"I. Want. You. And you're a terrible faker. You already knew."

"I know. But I've been rehearsing my shocked face."

"When did you know?"

"When you came out of Brian's hospital room. I had a vision of us sitting right here having this *exact* conversation."

"No, you didn't," I say, calling his bluff. He would have said something about the fact that we were sitting on the curb with police surrounding my house.

"You're right. When you went off to see Brian, I sat next to Jolene. She and I were talking about Elvin, and Lux, and *you*. We were watching the fish swimming around when I had this vision. It was foggy. I could barely make it out. But there we were, sitting on a porch, drinking lemonade, and holding hands. We're older. And, just so you know, I age exceptionally well."

"Your modesty is astounding," I say.

"I know. But it was *us*, and we were happy. I have no idea how we'll get to that point. Or *if* we'll get to that point, being that we're great at changing the future. I just hope that it happens."

"Can I see?"

"Sure."

I grab Mike's face in my hands and lower his head until our foreheads are touching. This worked last time, and I remember what Vanessa said about Mike and me being connected. She might be on to something.

I catch a glimpse of Mike's vision. He's right. It *is* foggy, which means it's not a future set in stone. We're in our sixties, maybe older, and we're sitting in rocking chairs with our hands interlocked, drinking lemonade and looking out at the sun setting behind the familiar hills surrounding Fernn Valley. If I'm not mistaken, there are several cats walking around and possibly kids, too. Grandkids, I would assume.

What I know for certain is that we look happy.

CHAPTER FIFTEEN

All the first responders are gone. All the bad guys are behind bars. All the good guys are alive. My work here is almost done. There's just the little matter of step three.

"Burn the lace curtains," Vanessa says. "The doll collection has to go. It screams *I'm nine!* Not, *I am a twenty-three-year-old mature woman with remarkable superpowers.* The walls should be white. Bright white. So white it almost hurts your eyes, and then do black furniture ... Are you texting or writing this down?"

I look up from my phone. "Writing this down."

"Good." Vanessa had moved *write article* to step four and made step three *makeover Zoe's room.* I was seven the last time my room was decorated. When she heard this, she sprang into action. "This daybed is atrocious. Honestly. I'm thinking you should move. What exactly do you do at *The Gazette*?"

"I write squirrel of the week and handle obituaries."

"How much do you make?"

"Not enough to survive on my own."

"Hmm." Vanessa taps her chin. "You can wait and see how your relationship with Brian goes. You might be ready to move in with him soon. You're lucky. I decorated his house, and it's fantastic. I have exceptional taste."

"I'm sure you do, but I'm with Mike."

Vanessa flickers as if she's shorting out. "Come again."

"I'm. With. Mike. I care for Brian, but I realized my feelings for him were based on my fantasies. What I feel for Mike is based on reality. Also, you compared Brian to Mr. Rogers, and that's how I think of my dad, and it ruined everything for me."

Vanessa doesn't even try to hide her delight. "This is the best news. And it's not because you kissed my boyfriend while I was dying and lied to me about it. It's because you and Mike make sense."

"Thank you."

"Does he have a home you can move into?"

"No. I'm not ready to move in with anyone yet, either." I sit on my bed and go to pet Jabba, who is sprawled out on my pillow, and he bites my hand. Which about sums up our relationship.

"That is one ugly cat," Vanessa says.

"I have this theory that he's actually the reincarnated spirit of a José Luis Francisco. He was a spirit I helped when I was three years old. I burned down our house while making him bacon. That's when my parents figured I was schizophrenic and it was best if I didn't socialize."

Vanessa's face is frozen in shock. "O-*kay* ... that's an ... *interesting* story. And one I wouldn't necessarily share with anyone else, ever. Anyway. We have a solid makeover plan for your room. Make sure to stick to my list, and you created a Pinterest account, right?"

"Right."

"Good. Let's write this piece."

It takes a full day to craft *the most compelling piece of journalism ever written* per Vanessa. She talked while I typed, and she talks fast. She talked even faster once news of the "Fernn Valley Strangler" had caught national attention.

Over the last twenty-four hours, media outlets from all over the country have flocked to my small town to recount the tale of a seemingly quiet bowtie-wearing man who had been silently killing for years. The police uncovered bodies buried along the Paradise Falls Creek. So far, they are up to four ... and still digging.

He chose his victims well. Lolly, he made to look like a suicide. Brintley was a runaway. No one knew where she was. Another victim was a woman who had stayed at the bed and breakfast *years* ago, and she was driving through town, having just left her husband. This was before iPhones and social media. He'd chosen Lux, thinking she was a drifter.

How wrong he was.

I send the article to the editor-in-chief at the *Portland Times* with the subject line *Vanessa Tobin's last article. How she caught the Fernn Valley Strangler*. She'd managed to skillfully tell the story in a way that didn't reveal that most of the key pieces of investigation were done after she died. Instead, she wrote about the police dismissing Jolene's pleas for help. About discovering the secret tunnel in the Ishmaels' guest room closet. About how Gary Handhoff had run her off the tow yard property. About how he was under investigation for his involvement in destroying evidence for Elvin. About meeting me and our working together to find out it was Elvin. There is no mention of my gifts. It's written in a way that insinuates we met when she first came to Fernn Valley. There is also no mention of her death. Obviously, since she can't very well write an article if she's dead.

"I want you to put your name on it," she'd said before I'd hit *send*. "By Vanessa Tobin and Zoe Lane. This is our story now." I was hesitant, but Vanessa was insistent. "This will open doors for you, hopefully bring in more income, and provide you the means to get out of this room."

Couldn't argue with that.

The editor responded immediately, and by noon the article was on the *Oregon Times* website and was trending on Twitter.

Side note: I now have a twitter, Instagram, Facebook, and Pinterest account, because I'm so modern like that.

My phone is blowing up with requests for interviews. I kindly decline all invitations to go on television. Being on national news sounds like my own personal hell. Jolene is not camera shy, and she's been on just about every news show there is, talking about her daughter and her killer and finding justice for Lux. Despite the horrid circumstance, she looks at peace.

I'm okay with over-the-phone interviews. And over the course of the next week, I do at least five a day.

"This is everything I always wanted," Vanessa says as soon as I hang up with the *Los Angeles Times*. She's spinning around my living room, and Jabba hisses at her. "Oh, shut up."

"That was the last of my interviews that I have scheduled." I curl up on the couch and pull a blanket over my legs. "Now, how do we submit this article for an award?"

"I have no idea what you're talking about."

"You said that you wanted to be an award-winning journalist. Don't you have to submit your article to a ... contest?" I have no idea how this works. Obviously.

"I've decided that going viral is better than winning an award. This step is complete."

"Wait." I stand up. "Are you leaving?"

"Looks like it."

"Now?"

She pauses to think. "Yep. I'm good. I'm really, really good. Tell Mike bye for me?"

"B-but, he'll be here soon. He's just at an open house with my parents."

"Zoe Lane." She clasps her hands over her heart. "I am ready to go. I'll hang out with my grandma. Maybe I'll look up Lux. She seems like good people."

"B-b-b-but ..."

"Zoe Lane, stop your stuttering. Be confident in your thoughts and words and abilities. And remember, emotional receptacle." Vanessa takes a step back. "I'd give you a hug, but I don't want to shock you."

I nod my head slowly.

Vanessa opens her arms, stares up at the ceiling, and *poof*.

She's gone.

CHAPTER SIXTEEN

Two months later ...

"All I'm saying is that we could have had something," Beth says.

I'm at work and Beth sits across from me. She's over sports. Desks are pushed together in groups of two in the workroom. I sit next to Brian's office, while Mike is all the way on the other side of the room by the window. He does IT, and he's busy doing ... whatever it is that IT people do.

It's weird being back at *The Gazette*, resuming our everyday tasks like nothing has changed. When in reality, everything has.

"He was so handsome and talented," Beth is still talking. "The way he moved his hips ... I think I was born in the wrong era." She rolls her chair over to my desk. "Please?"

"No, I am not contacting Elvis." I click Save on my *Squirrel of the Week* article. I named him Apple because he was eating an apple he'd stolen off the tree. I'd snapped the picture in Mike's backyard the day he moved into his new home.

He'd bought a little two bedroom off Crawford Street, not far from where Beth lives. The paint is chipped, the fireplace is falling apart, the carpet smells like urine, and the kitchen is in desperate need of a sledgehammer. But it has a magnificent back porch. I know that's what sealed the deal for Mike. Even if it's not the one from his vision.

We'd spent every night since escrow closed trashing the place. Smashing tile with a hammer is quite therapeutic. He's going for white walls with black accents. I have an entire Pinterest board dedicated to his remodel.

My mom nearly passed out from excitement when I told her about Mike and me. And I'm not exaggerating. She had to sit down and fan her face. My dad had to get her a cup of water. Even if she won't openly admit that I'm a medium, I know she knows. I also know that she was scared I'd spend my life alone. I mean, who wants to date someone who speaks to dead people?

We haven't told her about Mike's gifts yet. We're easing her into the paranormal world.

"Have you ever contacted any celebrities?" Beth asks.

"I don't know what you're talking about."

"Oh, please. Everyone in town knows about you."

She's right. Not everyone in town *believes* me. But everyone knows. "I don't contact celebrities or any former presidents," I say. "Now, if you have a relative that you'd like to talk to, I may be able to help."

"For a price," says Mike, walking up with his laptop open. "Check this out. I added a header." He's been working on a website for the last month, convinced we should take our medium duo on the road.

I'm not sure anyone will pay us. I'm not sure I *want* anyone to pay us. That's a lot of pressure, and I feel bad taking money from those who are grieving. But I'm letting Mike do his thing.

"We'll put *This is for entertainment purposes only* on the bottom," he had said. "It's what all the psychics and mediums put on their websites to prevent getting sued."

Whatever.

"Looks good," says Beth. "Are you going to charge friends and co-workers for your services?"

"Yes," says Mike. "No," I say.

"Mike." I give him a playful shove.

He mocks hurt. "What? I have a mortgage now, and a girlfriend who has expensive decorating taste."

I laugh, because he's right. Pinterest is a dangerous place for me.

The door to Brian's office opens. "Zoe and Mike. Can I talk to you for a minute?" he asks.

Mike closes his laptop and gives me a *what does he want with the both of us* look. I don't know why he is asking me. He's the one who can see the future.

We step into Brian's office, and he closes the door behind us. It's still a little awkward to be around Brian and Mike at the same time. My feelings for Brian didn't evaporate the moment I chose Mike. However, I'm happy, and Brian understands. He needed time to mourn and process all that he'd been through before he could jump into another relationship anyway.

"I have a job for your powers," Brian says.

"We like to call them gifts," says Mike.

"Sorry. I didn't mean to offend you."

"No offense taken," I say.

Brian adjusts his glasses. "I just got word that Mr. Sanders was found dead this morning at the pharmacy."

Oh, no. "A heart attack?" I ask, remembering how he didn't handle the shock from Vanessa very well. "His son is getting married this Saturday. How horrible for the entire family."

"It wasn't a heart attack. He's been shot, and Mrs. Ishmael is in custody."

You could knock me over with a feather. "Mrs. Ishmael?"

"Is this about the cat?" asks Mike. "Dang, she can hold a grudge."

"I don't think she killed him," Brian says. "I can't imagine her shooting anyone. It's not in her character."

I agree.

"So." He looks at us expectantly. "Can you do your ... thing? Is he here?"

Mike looks off into the distance and shakes his head. "I got nada. What about you, Lane?"

I close my eyes and summon Mr. Sanders. A chill runs down my spine, and my fingertips go numb. When I lift my lids, I can see my breath huff out in a cloud.

A man appears behind Brian's desk. He's young and lean and wearing red tweed pants, a white collared shirt with red stripes, and a red tie with yellow polka dots. His dark hair is sprayed into a helmet, and his mustache covers his top lip.

This can't possibly be, "Mr. Sanders?"

"Yes. It's me!" He spins in a slow circle with his arms out, admiring his young physique. "I'm in my twenties again. Don't I look great? I forgot what a stud I was."

It sure was nice having peace and quiet while it lasted.

The End

A NOTE FROM ERIN

Hello! I want to personally thank you. Yes, YOU, the one with the book/phone/Kindle/tablet in your hand. I appreciate you taking the time out of your busy life to read *The Marvelous Ms. Medium*.

If you enjoyed the book, it would make my day if you left a review on Amazon. I'd also like to invite you to join my mailing list to stay up to date on my latest news and special sales, and get a free ebook of *Can't Pay My Rent*! You can sign up at: http://bit.ly/erinhussnews

The next book in the series will be *The Medium Tale.* Mr. Sanders has been a blast to write, and his murder takes a hilarious turn. Brian is joining the investigation this time, and there's a twist even I didn't see coming! Information regarding release date and pre-order coming soon. Until then, I have the Cambria Clyne Mystery Series published by Gemma Halliday that I think you'll enjoy. As always, the best way to keep up to date on my newest releases is to signup for my newsletter or follow me on social media. I'm especially active on Instagram, and I love hearing from my readers.

My sincerest thanks,
Erin

ABOUT THE AUTHOR

Erin Huss is a blogger and a #1 Kindle bestselling author. Erin shares hilarious property management horror stories at The Apartment Manager's Blog and her own horror stories at erinhuss.com. She currently resides in Southern California with her husband and five children, where she complains daily about the cost of living but will never do anything about it.

ROCKY ROAD & REVENGE

Book #2 in the award-winning Cambria Clyne Mystery Series

PROLOGUE

We all lie. You know it. I know it. If we're being watched by shape-shifting Lizard People, like every conspiracy theorist on Hollywood Boulevard thinks we are, then they know it too. Most are the daily lies we tell ourselves—*I can eat this cookie now because I'm starting a diet on Monday,* or *I'll shave my legs tomorrow*, or *two Diet Cokes for breakfast is totally normal.*

Other lies are disguised as secrets. Like when Tam in Apartment 7 tells his wife he's going for a run but really he's behind the maintenance garage playing Clash Royale on his phone. For me, it's the stash of Thin Mints I have hidden in my nightstand under *Pride and Prejudice*, which I've never read, never plan to. I watched the movie, once. Just so I could hold my own should I find myself in a social situation where Mr. Darcy is the topic of conversation. Which has yet to happen. Nineteenth-century literature doesn't do it for me.

For the record: eating Thin Mints does.

Some lies are earth-shattering. Like Trent's in Apartment 23. Every workday at exactly 11:15 AM a brunette in tight pants knocks on his door. Trent answers, plunges his tongue down her throat, let's her inside the apartment, and she exits an hour later looking quite pleased and mighty disheveled. Trent is married to a blonde. A blonde who thinks he's at home working all day.

Then there are the deadly lies. I'm talking if-you-knew-the-truth-I'd-have-to-kill- you type of lies. This is what makes my job interesting. As an apartment manager, I'm privy to all the secrets, all the omissions, and all the lies my residents tell. Whether I want to be or not.

It's not a job for the squeamish, hotheaded, or those with a heart condition. It's a job for me...or at least I thought it was, until I had to crawl through a burning building with a dog on my chest and bullets whizzing over my head.

Now, I'm not so sure. I hear phlebotomy is a nice profession.

CHAPTER ONE

Property manager (n): *the person charged with the care of a real estate property. See also: Firefighter*

There was an urn on my desk. It wasn't one of those giant vase-looking urns, like the one my Grandma Ruthie's ashes were kept in. This one was subtle, looked more like a decoration than an urn. It was a shiny mahogany box engraved with *Mom* in swirly letters along with little flowers—forget-me-nots, if I wasn't mistaken. Ironic, since Mom had most certainly been forgotten.

I'd found the urn early that morning after a move-out inspection. Steph Woo, the now former resident of Apartment 17, was supposed to meet me at 7:00 AM for a walk- through but never showed up. Probably because her walls were painted

Pepto pink and the place smelled like corn. There was little hope for a security deposit refund. She'd left the urn in her carport cabinet. I didn't know what else to do with it, so I put it on my desk and left Steph a message to come pick it up.

My name is Cambria Clyne. I'm an on-site apartment manager slash caretaker of the cremated and forgotten.

"Congratulations. You're now cursed," Amy said when I called later to tell her about my latest move-out find.

I leaned close to my computer and plugged one ear to better hear Amy over the residents passing through the lobby. "How am I cursed?"

"Harboring an urn that doesn't belong to you disturbs the deceased and causes bad luck," she said, as if this were public knowledge.

"Are you sure that's a real thing?"

"It's most certainly a real thing. You should have left it where you found it or put it in that closet by the pool. The one with all the other crap people forgot when they moved."

"If I were dead, being shoved into a storage closet would disturb me more than being placed on a desk."

"Well, you're not dead, and you have no idea how these things work." Aside from being my best friend, Amy was also an actress. She had recently landed the role of the sultry medium, Page Harrison, on the prime-time drama *Ghost Confidential* and spent much of her spare time researching the hereafter in the name of character development.

"I'm sure Steph will be back shortly to claim her mom, and all will be right in the spiritual world again," I said.

"Let's hope so. The last thing you need is bad luck." This was true. "Also, who forgets their mom?" "Maybe she set it on the shelf while she loaded the car, and forgot it?" I said. "See, that's the problems with urns. They're too portable. For the record, when I die, please have me buried at Westwood Memorial. I can't risk being misplaced." "You don't want to be buried back home?" "Are you kidding me? Do not bury me in Fresno. I belong in Los Angeles," she

said. "There's better weather here."

"I don't think weather matters too much when you're dead. Also, Westwood is where Marilyn Monroe is buried, and Hugh Hefner, and Natalie Wood, and Farrah Fawcett and—"

"Are you on Wikipedia?" "Maybe." *Yes.* "It sounds like a pricey place to decompose." "That's fine. Pick a space no one wants by the fence or the freeway." "Why are we even talking about this?" I asked. "Are you planning to die soon?" "No, but one can never be too prepared." She exhaled into the receiver. "Anyway,

I'm done shooting for the day. I'm coming by. I have to tell you about what happened to me last night, and I'll see what I can do about the urn situation."

"You realize you're not a real medium, right?" The line went silent. "Hello?" I glanced down at my phone's home screen: a picture of my daughter,

Lilly, and me on New Year's Eve with party horns in our mouths. Amy was gone.

I attempted a sigh. Except the dress I had on didn't offer much give for things like bending or moving or breathing or sighing. I wore it because the rusty color looked good against my pale, freckly skin, accentuated Einstein (my nickname for the dark mass of craziness springing from my head), and made my blue eyes pop.

OK, fine.

I typically wore jeans, Converse, and a T-shirt to work, but it was laundry day, and the dress was the only clean item in my closet that fit—and I use the word *fit* loosely. Or should I say *tightly*. I'd been eating my feelings as of late. I had a lot of feelings to get through. My feelings tasted like rocky road ice cream.

Whatever. I didn't have time to worry about belly rolls, spirit disturbances, or silly superstitions. I had work to do. There was a property inspection coming up, and everything had to be perfect.

Once I had a year of property management under my belt, I planned to apply for a position at a more prominent complex, one with hundreds of units, leasing agents, a full maintenance staff, and a golf cart. In my mind, if you need a golf cart to get from one end of the property to the next, you've made it.

The best way to achieve golf-cart-status was to impress the property trustee with my reports and pristine grounds and, of course, make my boss look good. These were Patrick's exact words when he called the day before to remind me that "The McMills own ninety percent of my company's portfolio. This meeting on Thursday must run smoothly. I don't want any surprises. Please make Elder Property Management look good." I got the message loud and clear and was happy to report everything was in order. The meeting would run smoothly. I would impress the trustee. All I had to do was keep it together for the next forty-eight hours, and that golf cart was as good as mine.

Next on my to-do list: the lobby.

I fluffed the couch pillows, adjusted the armchairs just so, wiped down the glass coffee table until I could see my reflection, and vacuumed the carpet. The lobby had been decorated sometime in the late eighties and not touched since. Lots of florals. Lots of stripes. Lots of neon colors. Busy wallpaper. Teal carpet. Yellow linoleum. Eucalyptus branches.

The eighties was not a good decade for home furnishings.

I'd put together a proposal to redecorate. My plan was to fuse the patterns and colors from the seventies with the deco furnishings found in many Los Angeles homes today. I thought it was an ingenious design (if I do say so myself). We *were* located in Los Angeles, and the building *was* constructed sometime in the seventies.

In my proposed revamp we'd have sleek furniture, abstract art, palms, and an orange accent wall. Patrick nearly fainted when I showed him the design. He told me it wasn't in the budget and even if it were, he'd never paint a wall orange.

So I was stuck with teal carpet and an overstuffed peach couch.

At least the lobby would smell good. I'd bought a wax warmer at Walmart and plugged it in next to the couch. It was in the shape of an owl and came with three scents. Cinnamon, linen, and apple pie.

Cinnamon was too Christmassy. Linen smelled like deodorant. Apple pie reminded me of, well, an apple pie.

Who doesn't love apple pie?

I placed three wax cubes on the tray and watched them turn to liquid. The sweet artificial scent filled the room. I grabbed my water bottle from the desk, took a seat on the ugly couch, and crossed my legs. It was quiet. Lilly had gone with her dad, Tom, for the day, and it was near closing time, which meant most residents would use the pedestrian gate instead of walking through the lobby.

I threw my hands behind my head, sat back, and had a look around. Sure the lobby was offensive to the eyes, but it was home, and the perfect setup for a single mom like myself. To the right was my enclosed office with a waist-high counter (also teal, also ugly) overlooking the lobby, where I could work and chat with the residents who walked through. The door behind my desk opened to my attached two-bedroom apartment. I could be working one minute, turn around, step into the kitchen, and make— *That doesn't smell right?*

***

Random fact: if a wax warmer catches on fire, dousing it with water causes a *bigger* fire. Also, 1980s furniture is quite flammable.

The emergency service personnel hustled to and from the wreckage while I watched the scene unfold from the street. "Mom" was safe in my hands. I'd wrapped the urn in a sweatshirt for protection before I rushed out of the building. If moving an urn disturbed the deceased, then lighting one on fire could have eternal consequences. Not that I really believed in all that.

It didn't take long for a group of residents to congregate on the driveway. Their breaths huffed out in white clouds against the darkening sky as they chattered about their manager, who had just burned down the building. Which technically wasn't true. The building was still erect. The lobby was just a bit crispy now. However, Silvia Kravitz stood in the middle of the crowd with her parrot, Harold, perched on her shoulder, and by this time tomorrow I'd be a pyromaniac who burned down the building.

Silvia was the Mayor of Rumorville, with Harold as her deputy. She'd started a rumor last year that I had a threesome with the retired couple in Apartment 22. You could read all about it on Yelp, Apartment Ratings, Rent or Run dot com, and *Superior Senior Living*.

So now I was a pyromaniac with a geriatric fetish.

Meh.

I'd been called worse.

I approached the group of residents on shaky legs. My nerves were fried. Silvia folded her arms and tapped her foot. Silvia Kravitz was a retired actress who looked like the seventy-year-old love child of Gollum and Joan Rivers. And she only wore lingerie: no matter the time of day, the occasion, or whether or not the sun was at the perfect angle to blast through the sheer fabric.

"A faulty wax warmer caught fire, and the damage was contained to the lobby," I said to them. "No apartments were involved."

"What about smoke inhalation?" Silvia said with a theatrical wave of her hand.

Harold turned his backside to me. Everyone standing around her nodded and whispered "good point" to each other.

"Excuse me?"

Silvia draped an arm around Shanna, the new resident in Apartment 15. "This poor young dear has an audition tomorrow, and how is she to sing with smoke-filled lungs?"

Shanna let out a dainty cough. Heaven help me. I had too many actors in my life. I assured everyone the best way to avoid smoke inhalation was to go home and

close the doors. Two out of fifteen residents listened to their property manager. Which was about the national average.

As the firefighters left and the trucks disappeared, the crowd eventually thinned. Residents lost interest and went back to their apartments. Which was good, because I still had to call Patrick.

He freaked.

"Look at the couch!" I had him on FaceTime so he could see the damage for himself. The fire inspector had deemed the structure sound and allowed me back in. The office was smoky but not charred. My apartment was smelly but fine. Other than that, it wasn't so bad.

OK, fine. That's a lie.

It was terrible. I had the trustee inspection in two days, and I'd just burned down the lobby! The back wall was singed, the couch unrecognizable, the beams were exposed, ash rained down, the once teal carpet was black, and firefighters had busted one window.

At least no one was hurt, and the lobby would get a new look after all? I had to find the silver lining to keep from crying. "It's a nightmare!" Patrick wasn't a silver-lining kind of guy. "You'll need to board

the window and call the insurance, and we'll need a restoration company out there tonight."

"Done. Done, and done," I said. "The restoration company will be here in an hour. I left a message with the claims department, and Mr. Nguyen is out buying wood for the window." Mr. Nguyen was the maintenance man. We couldn't pronounce his first name, so we kept it formal. "You don't have to worry. I'll take care of everything." I gave what I hoped was a reassuring smile.

Patrick responded with a grunt. We hung up with a promise that I wouldn't burn anything else down.

I sighed the best I could in my restrictive clothing. What a mess. I picked up a seared throw pillow with my forefinger and thumb. My eyes cut over to "Mom." She was back on the desk, sitting between the stapler and the ancient answering machine. I thought about what Amy had said...

Before I could dwell too much on the paranormal, Chase showed up. Chase Cruller (as in the donut) was once the maintenance man. He was now a detective for the great city of Los Angeles. Which kept him busy. There were a lot of criminals around these parts.

Chase was also *sort of* my boyfriend. He has dark blond hair, green eyes, a five o'clock shadow no matter the time of day, rock-solid abs, and I'm pretty sure he could be an underwear model if he weren't busy fighting bad guys.

He sidestepped the debris to avoid dirtying his shiny shoes. He had on a gray tailored suit and black tie, the outfit reserved for super-official detective duty.

"What are you doing here?" I asked him.

"I saw the fire trucks driving down Sepulveda and had a strange hunch they were coming from your place." He looked around, taking in the new landscape of the lobby. "What happened?"

"The wax warmer caught on fire, so I doused it with my water, and it caught on fire more."

"That's unfortunate." He brushed a fallen ash off his sleeve.

"Very. So why are you so formal?" I tugged on the lapels of his jacket "Funeral or press conference?"

"Press conference?" Chase narrowed his eyes. "You haven't heard the news?" "Been a little busy." I waved to the crispy lobby. "Why? What happened?" "Jessica Wilders was murdered." I gasped.

"Her assistant found her at home this morning with multiple gunshot wounds." I gasped. "Wasn't pretty." Jessica Wilders was the star of *Ghost Confidential.* Amy would argue there was

no "star," that it was an ensemble, but that was only because she couldn't stand Jessica— who was the star. Jessica was a skeletal brunette with dark eyes and a gap between her two front teeth—what she was known for. She played Lola Darling, a ghost trapped in the body of her ex-husband's new wife, who was also her killer's sister. It was gripping television.

I'd met Jessica at a cast party once. I'd tagged along as Amy's last-minute date. Her boyfriend had to work late because "he's a *doc-tor*," Amy had announced upon arrival. About thirty minutes into the night, I'd managed a short but meaningful conversation with Jessica. She asked me where the bathroom was because she thought I worked there. Too starstruck to form words, I pointed a crab leg toward the commodes. This was the extent of our interaction, and now she was dead.

"That's horrible. Do you have any idea who killed her?" I asked Chase. "No suspects and no solid leads right now, but we'll get there," he said. I wondered how Amy had taken the news. Come to think of it...*where is Amy?*

She said she was coming over, and that was hours ago.

Chase checked his watch. "I have to head to the station now. This is the highest- profile case I've ever worked so..."

"I'll see you when I see you." I hid my disappointment with a smile. "No worries. Go catch the killer, and I'll be here, trying not to burn anything else down."

Chase pulled me closer and tucked a strand of Einstein behind my ear. "Thank you for understanding."

"Of course." I wrapped my arms around his waist. I could feel the holster on his hip. I'm not going to lie—knowing he was packing heat was kind of hot. "You can make it up to me later."

"Oh yeah?" A devilish grin spread across his face. "What did you have in mind?"

"Gee, I don't know. Let me think about it." I played coy. The man knew what I wanted.

Chase leaned in and kissed me. His stubble was rough against my face, but his lips were sweet and firm. My legs went to goo.

"Is this what you had in mind?" he whispered against my mouth.

"Actually, I was going to say ice cream, pizza, and the latest Liam Neeson movie, but this is a good start."

Chase laughed. "I'll call you tomorrow." "You better." I gave him a playful smack on the rear. Chase sidestepped the debris on his way to the door, when in came Tom, with

Lilly at his side. Oh geez.

Tom Dryer (as in the appliance) was my one-night-stand turned baby daddy. He was a criminal defense attorney. Does mostly pro bono work. Which kept him busy. There were a lot of poor criminals around these parts.

If you squinted and tilted your head to the side, Tom looked like a tall Dylan McDermott. He could probably be an underwear model too. My parents thought he was gay. But the hundred or so women he'd slept with over the course of his lifetime would attest otherwise.

Tom was wearing basketball shorts, a Lakers tee, sandals, and a frown.

He wasn't my *sort of* boyfriend. Tom didn't do relationships. There were feelings there. He knew it. I knew it. Chase knew it. No one talked about it. Which made this reunion *sort of* awkward.

Blissfully unaware of the tension in the air, Lilly ran up and wrapped her arms around my legs. I swung her on my hip and gave her a kiss on the cheek. "What happens to the lobby?" she asked.

"What *happened* was there was a fire." I swept a dark curl off her forehead. "There were *three* fire trucks here."

Lilly's hazel eyes went wide. "Did you get to ride in one?" "Not this time." "Wow, Cam." Tom stepped in further and stood beside Chase. They

acknowledged each other with a quick jerk of their chins. "You OK?" "I'm fine. It was a silly mishap." I giggled what was supposed to be an endearing

giggle but sounded more like an old-lady cackle. 'Cause I'm smooth like that. "Oh no!" Lilly slapped her forehead. "Are my dolls OK?" "I think they are. Why don't you go check."

Lilly scrambled to break free from my grasp and ran into the apartment. The situation became fifty times more uncomfortable without the toddler buffer around.

"So..." I rocked from heel to toe. "How 'bout them Dodgers?"

Chase shoved his hands into the front pocket of his slacks. "They choked in the World Series."

"I hardly call losing in game seven a choke job."

I'd forgotten how much Tom loved his Dodgers. And how much Chase didn't love the Dodgers. He was an Angels fan.

Bad icebreaker. "Um...so, Jessica Wilders is dead." 'Cause murder is a better icebreaker? Honestly. *Note to self: you suck at icebreakers.* "I heard about that." Tom turned to Chase. "Are you working the case?" Chase nodded his head. "That should take up a lot of your time." Tom perked up and looked at me. "I'll

call you tomorrow." Oh geez. I had no idea how to handle so much male attention. I pulled at my collar. "You know what? I have to clean up this mess and call Amy

to be sure she's OK." I ushered the two outside. "Thank you for stopping by. Take care. Talk to you

later." I closed the door and locked it, which did little good since the window was missing and I could hear the two arguing baseball outside.

I grabbed my phone and called Amy. It went straight to voicemail. Even if Amy and Jessica Wilders didn't get along, I knew Amy would be devastated. I tried calling her again. It went straight to voicemail.

I sent a text.

Heard about Jessica. Are you OK?

Get the book at erinhuss.com

Made in the USA
Middletown, DE
15 April 2025